FACE OF THE EARTH, HEART OF THE SKY

Bilingual Press/Editorial Bilingüe

General Editor
  Gary D. Keller

Managing Editor
  Karen S. Van Hooft

Associate Editors
  Karen Akins Swartz
  Barbara H. Firoozye

Assistant Editor
  Linda St. George Thurston

Editorial Board
  Juan Goytisolo
  Francisco Jiménez
  Eduardo Rivera
  Mario Vargas Llosa

Address:
  Bilingual Press
  Hispanic Research Center
  Arizona State University
  P.O. Box 872702
  Tempe, Arizona 85287-2702
  (480) 965-3867

FACE OF THE EARTH, HEART OF THE SKY

Mario Roberto Morales

Translated from the Spanish by Edward Waters Hood

Bilingual Press/Editorial Bilingüe

TEMPE, ARIZONA

ISBN 0-927534-88-6

Library of Congress Cataloging-in-Publication Data

Morales, Mario Roberto, 1947–
    [Señores bajo los árboles. English]
    Face of the earth, heart of the sky / Mario Roberto
Morales ; translation by Edward Waters Hood.
        p.   cm.
    ISBN 0-927534-88-6 (alk. paper)
        I. Hood, Edward W. (Edward Waters), 1954–   II. Title.

PQ7499.2.M65 S4613 1999
863—dc21   99-047067

PRINTED IN THE UNITED STATES OF AMERICA

Cover design, interior by John Wincek, Aerocraft Charter Art Service
Back cover photo by Mayari Morales

Acknowledgments

Part of this work was first published in *The Literary Review,* vol.
41, no 1 (Fall 1997) with the title "Scenes of Lake Atitlán."

Partial funding provided by the Arizona Commission on the
Arts through appropriations from the Arizona State Legislature
and grants from the National Endowment for the Arts.

*To all those here that speak their word to the Face of the Sky,
to the Face of the Earth, in the Quincentennial Anniversary
of the encounter with the Men of the Mirrors, those of the
Floating Houses, the Metallic Bearded ones with Fire in their
Arms, those with four feet and two heads, the ballasts and dregs
of Spain. And upon the tenth anniversary (1992) of the beginning of the worst.*

"Then the Xibalbás laughed again. Their tongues were thick with laughter; the serpent Laughter was born in their heart, in their blood, in their bones. They laughed; all the Xibalbás laughed."

Popul Vuh

"O brave one, Male, Prisoner, Captive. Is this how your voice spoke to the Face of the Sky, to the Face of the Earth? . . ."
"O Eagles! O Jaguars! Come then and complete your mission, carry out your duty; may your teeth, your claws, kill me in an instant, because I am a Male from the mountains, from the valleys. May the Heavens and the Earth be with You. O Eagles! O Jaguars!"

Rabinal Achí

"The women that sing, the men that sing, and all those that sing shall be dispersed throughout the Earth. The child sings, the old man sings, the old woman sings, the young man sings, the young woman sings."

The Book of the Books of Chilam Balam

". . . the Spaniards made a law, that all the Indians of each sex and age they took alive be thrown into holes in the ground. The same with pregnant women and those that had given birth, children and elders, and as many as they could capture they threw into the holes until they overflowed, stakes passed through their bodies. It was particularly terrible to see the women with their children. They killed the rest of them with lances and knives, they set attack dogs on them that tore them to pieces and devoured them . . . . They continued this inhuman butchery for nearly seven years."

Bartolomé de las Casas

"The oppressors and the oppressed finally meet, and the only thing still true is that life was too short for both."

Don Juan Matus

AUTHOR'S NOTE

All the voices in this book are real. Its fictional character resides in the artistic transformation of these voices into a structure and language that are not real, were never real, nor have any reason to have been real.

I did not bother to disguise the stories or the voices very much. This is a case in which reality overwhelms fiction to such a degree that the latter must serve the former with appropriate humility. Therefore, this book belongs to its protagonists.

TRANSLATOR'S NOTE

Although Guatemala, the setting of this testimonial novel, shares some traits with other Central American nations, it is unique in many ways. The country is characterized by the presence of two distinct and complex cultures, the Ladino and the indigenous, as well as their innumerable articulations. The Ladino culture is an emerging hybrid consisting of European and indigenous elements; the indigenous culture consists of twenty-two different ethnicities of Maya origin, peoples who have resisted political and cultural domination in their ancient homelands since the days of the Spanish Conquest. These two broad groups constitute, in approximately equal parts, the population of modern Guatemala.

In *Face of the Earth, Heart of the Sky* (original title *Señores bajo los árboles*), Mario Roberto Morales demonstrates the talented, experimental approach evidenced in three previous award-winning novels: *Obraje* ("Workplace," Premio Centroamericano de Novela, 1971), *Los demonios salvajes* ("Wild Devils," Premio Único Centroamericano de Novela, 1977), and *El esplendor de la pirámide* ("Splendor of the Pyramid," Premio Latinoamericano de Narrativa, 1985). Without resorting to simplistic ideological or literary categories, Morales presents in his texts a strong condemnation of recent social and political events in his homeland. *Señores bajo los árboles*, a testimonial novel (or *testinovela*, as Morales characterizes his text), treats the Guatemalan army's recent war on the country's indigenous peoples.

One of the most interesting aspects of the novel is its mixture of authentic testimonial texts with fictional ones. In a 1996 interview, Morales described the construction of *Señores bajo los árboles*:

> It's a book that I've threaded together, as it were—sewn together, stitched up, a book based on discursive pieces of indigenous accounts from the scorched earth in Guatemala. I brought the parts together into a linguistic whole with some fictional nexuses to give it continuity, to produce a literary work dealing with speech forms native people use when they express themselves in Spanish. Prior to that I had done some research that led me to discover some unknown *testimonios* and to rework other testimonies already published. That's how the book came together. (*South Eastern Latin Americanist* 15.1-2 [1996]: 41)

In *Señores bajo los árboles*, Morales intentionally appropriates materials from diverse testimonial, historical, and fictional texts to construct his vision of the recent war in Guatemala. One of these sources is *Harvest of Violence*—a collection of essays edited by Robert Carmack on the impact of the Guatemalan army's counterinsurgency campaign against the country's indigenous populations—a book that Morales translated into Spanish. This use of palimpsest establishes dialogues with other texts and gives an important intertextual and metatextual dimension to the work.

According to Morales, the *testinovela* is an emerging literary form in which fiction is used by the novelist in the service of testimonial truth. In a paper presented at the Tercer Congreso Internacional de Literatura Centroamericana held in Guatemala in February 1995, Morales described his book in the following manner: "*Señores bajo los árboles* aspires to be, in fiction, a modest hybrid proposal that, on an aesthetic/literary level, represents (inadequately, as we know) the cultural and political hybridization of Guatemala in an especially cruel moment of its development." Morales also suggested that this literary project forms part of a model that could serve in the resolution of Guatemala's great cultural and political problems. This model "proposes the implementation of cultural policies for a multicultural country that guarantee—through egalitarian cultural rights—the free exercise and development of all the cultures that comprise our mestizo ensemble. "

Structurally, the novel is divided into three sections: "First Fragments of the Explosion," "Other Fragments," "And More Fragments." In all, the novel consists of twenty-four fragments, including epigraphs from pre-Columbian religious texts, real *testimonios* of indigenous Guatemalans, directions for filming a documentary on Lake Atitlán, excerpts from a military training manual, and fragments of a fictional plot about the life of Toribio de León, an Indian boy who is forcefully recruited by the Guatemalan army after his father is burned to death. He becomes a *kaibil*, one of the elite forces employed by the Guatemalan government in their conflict against leftist guerrillas. Morales employs the fictional plot along with the testimonial texts to document the Guatemalan army's campaign of terror against indigenous communities during the early eighties, but he also holds the guerrilla movement partly responsible for the massacres. Tragically, Guatemala's natives became the victims in the conflict between the guerrillas and the army, a dynamic not without precedents.

Morales's most recent narrative texts include *El ángel de la retaguardia*, 1997 ("Rearguard Angel"), and *Los que se fueron por la libre*, 1998 ("They Did It Their Own Way").

* * *

In order to maintain the integrity of the unique universe that forms the referent for this text, many Spanish and Mayan terms have been left in their original form. For example, the Spanish term *compañero*, which means friend or companion, has been retained as well as the abbreviated form *compa*, which in Central

America was used among revolutionaries and guerrilla fighters to refer to a member of their military or political organizations. In addition, proper names, for example those referring to the Mayan ethnicities, have not been altered. The five indigenous groups mentioned in the novel are the Quichés, Cackchiqueles, Tzutuhiles, Kekchíes, and Mames. English equivalents for the Spanish and indigenous terms are found in a glossary at the end of the novel.

When this book was published in Guatemala in 1994, controversies arose regarding the technique employed in its writing, which consisted of stitching together authentic voices of indigenous people affected by the wars of insurgency and counterinsurgency. Some went so far as to insinuate that there had been plagiarism, but that notion did not prosper, for obvious reasons. It was also said that I was not entitled to write about indigenous people because I am not an indigenous person. This notion was not given credence either, for the same reasons. The fiercest criticism came from the Guatemalan National Revolutionary Unity, because in the book indigenous voices denounce abuses committed by guerrilla forces from their organization as well as by the army, even though the book respects the differences in proportion and places almost all the blame for the dirty war on the army. I had to wait five years—until February 1999, when the Commission for Historical Clarification or Truth Commission made public in its final report the definitive version of events—for my book to be vindicated. Indeed, this report eventually corroborated that the guerrilla movement as well as the army committed atrocities against the civilian population, although the burden of guilt has fallen on the army for its criminal excesses.

With great satisfaction I can say that the version the reader has in hand may be considered, for the aforementioned reasons, a fictionalization of historic truth. With it I settle an old account with the ruling elites of my country, who made a peace treaty conceived as a mechanism to cover up their crimes and to co-govern with impunity. Today the left and the right play democratic politics without seeking changes that might benefit the majority, making the signing of the peace accords the greatest historic fraud committed against the Guatemalan people since the overthrow of President Arbenz in 1954.

The Author

I

FIRST FRAGMENTS OF THE EXPLOSION

W hen a baby is born its umbilical cord and placenta are gathered and carried to the place known as the foundation behind the temascal, or sacred steam bath. There it is buried, to the right side of the temascal or chuj if it is from a boy and to the left if it is from a girl, until twenty days pass. When that time has passed, the copal is prepared; it is mashed and wrapped in tree leaves. Two hens are made ready. The head is chopped off one of them and its blood is poured on the copal. Then the medicine man takes confession from the man, that is from the father of the baby. The confession ceremony begins in his house. They chant and place the little pouches of copal on the newborn baby. The shamans have a brazier, a pine cross, and a seedling, also two stones brought from the chuj, the kind that are heated, and which water is poured on to produce vapor. Everything is painted with the hen's blood and carried to a place near water where it is buried, and candles are placed there that later must be carried to the church to be placed at the feet of the Saint. That day the baby's godparents come to feast. A lamb is slaughtered, the atole drink called pusunque is prepared, and the godmother feeds the baby slowly, wetting her finger so it will suck. While doing this the godmother says prayers so that the baby will not be a gossiper.

The army arrives in waves, appearing on the plain, rising above the lowest hills. From the village a handful of small black points that blend in with the shadows of the clouds can be seen. Covered with leaves, the army rises in camouflage uniforms and stained faces. The army has many faces. It appears by the hill and by the river. It arrives on the road and suddenly has surrounded the village. Beneath the broken sky of early morning or the darkness of nightfall the army approaches. They (those from the army) arrive with black paint on their faces. They appear with torches in their hands. They burn our homes so that the people will come out and the children run screaming and the elders trip on the stones and the women cannot lift their children to their backs. They corral the men in the center of the village to kill them and lock the women in the church to rape them. They disembowel the children; they pull them from the slings on their mothers' backs and, grabbing them by their feet, smash them against the stones. They cut open the women's bellies, remove their little ones who have not even been born and throw them to the dogs after splitting them in two, ripping their legs apart like crabs. They appear, heading along the road, over the hill, through the plain. What do they want? What are they looking for now? . . .

he procession dispersed on time and spread out across the plaza. It climbed to the atrium of the church and crossed the entrances of the town hall. The fireworks maker Toribio de León and his friends ran about dressed as Moors, as Christians—blond, rose colored conquerors—and as wild animals, with their colored masks and their garments full of little mirrors and sequins. Toribio was dressed as a coyote.

The bottle rockets he and his father had made exploded in the sky without failing, as did the rockets they had delivered a week earlier to Father Aníbal for the celebration. The entire plaza was enshrouded in clouds of white smoke. The star-filled, late-afternoon sky was lit up from time to time by the exploding fireworks, and Toribio watched contentedly as the candy vendor—with his cargo of sweets on his back—enjoyed himself contemplating the light show in the sky and the points of the bell towers that still retained a little of the dying light of the afternoon sun. "Lollipops, lollipops, buy some lollipops! . . ."

Toribio had to help Chalío, the sacristan, light the fuses of the rockets with a hot coal. At the base of the mortar, the fuse protruded, almost touching the ground. One had to light it, get away, and hear the crack of the first explosion on land. Then, before the second explosion in the sky, Toribio—wearing his coyote mask—placed another rocket in the mouth of the mortar and drew the coal up next to the fuse, trying to make the explosions follow one another uninterruptedly. Then Chalío climbed the church tower and began to ring the bells. The fireworks, the tolling of bells, and everyone's laughter could not drown out the sacristan's shout from above. Making his way through the wall of people, his elderly voice reached all ears: "The army is coming! . . ." A silence descended, giving way to the noise of boots trampling underbrush and rifle bolts moving into firing position. The greenish ring of soldiers little by little began to close in upon the plaza. Cats, dogs, and birds became silent, and even the wind fled from the tree tops. Then a voice came over an electric megaphone. It said: "All of you in the procession, take off your masks!"

One by one the masks came down, revealing in their place many pairs of scurrying eyes and gaping mouths. Don Angel María, standing in the atrium beside Father Aníbal, watched as his son Toribio removed his coyote mask and slowly dropped the coal.

"All of you men, go to the side of the church!" thundered the electrified voice. "The women, to the side of the town hall, and the children to the top of the bandstand!"

From the top of the bell tower, Chalío watched the mass of people move. Neither Father Aníbal nor Don Angel María had to take a step because they were already standing in the place the voice had indicated. Toribio walked to the spot and stopped next to his father. The candy vendor also accompanied him: "Lollipops, lollipops! Pineapple for the girl, blackberry for the lady. . . ."

One group of soldiers went to the center of the plaza and, standing back to back, aimed their guns at the crowd. The circle was double: the people had bayonets at their backs and at their chests. The officer in charge walked in silence with the loudspeaker in his hand. He left the ranks of the troops, crossed the plaza, and climbed the bandstand where the children were. He caressed the heads of some of them and raised the loudspeaker to his mouth:

"We are here for our quota!" he shouted. Some of the boys, with their masks still in their hands, mumbled nervously. "Those who are eighteen years or older step forward! The army and the fatherland need you!"

For an instant it seemed that none of the boys was going to step forward, but little by little the sound of their shawls, mirrors, rattles, and sequins mingled with the noise of bare feet over the soil.

"No tricks—we're in no mood to waste time!" the officer shouted.

Toribio looked at his father, who, with a slight gesture, indicated for him to step forward. Suddenly two boys tried to flee: a group of soldiers went after them and a few moments later brought them back, dragging them and striking them on their heads with rifle butts. The officer's voice again thundered from the megaphone:

"The punishment for refusing to serve the fatherland is death. So, choose: either military service or the firing squad, right here and now!"

The crowd huddled together, murmuring. Smothered cries died in their shawls and the slings used to carry their children.

"Choose! Those who prefer military service, take one step forward; those who prefer the firing squad, stay where you are!"

Wearily, in unison, they stepped forward slowly, in humiliation and defeat. Toribio watched the blood drip down his friends' faces as the officer's voice ordered:

"Lieutenant, take their names, have all of them grab their stuff and climb on the truck!"

While his order was being carried out, the officer took a small notebook from his pocket and read: "The fireworks maker Angel María de León, the priest Aníbal Serrano, and the sacristan Chalío Matute, step forward!"

Don Angel María muttered almost inaudibly to his son not to speak, and he walked with Father Aníbal to the center of the plaza. Chalío remained up in the bell tower, huddled up like a small child beneath the mouth of the largest bell. As he walked towards the military truck, Toribio observed the candy vendor slip through the crowd: "Lollipops, lollipops: pineapple! . . ."

"That sacristan!" shouted the officer. "So old and such a coward! Bring him down from the bell tower now!"

Old Chalío, frozen with terror, was dragged down the stairs and lined up next to Don Angel María and Father Aníbal. Then the officer continued:

"The fatherland charges these three characters with subversion. The priest is a collaborator with the guerrillas. The fireworks maker organizes the cooperatives under orders from the priest according to instructions from the subversives, and the sacristan takes orders back and forth for the guerrillas and the priest. Those so-called cooperatives are only a front for

drawing people into the subversion. These men have been condemned by the fatherland to die. Therefore, say goodbye to
them and don't think of following their bad example, because
you could end up the way they have! Sergeant, proceed!"

The sergeant and two soldiers carried a can of gasoline to
the steps of the church; they opened it and poured its contents
over the heads and feet of the three men. Don Angel María again
signaled with his eyes to Toribio, who was lining up with his
friends, not to say anything. The sergeant and his men took out
boxes of matches; each lit one and threw it at the wet feet of the
three men. The faces of the whole community were illuminated
when the three men—on fire and shaking their arms like
babies—took several small steps backwards and forwards
before falling to their knees. They crawled around on all fours
and remained face up. They turned black and curled up as the
fire began to die down. The crowd remained silent, smelling the
stench of burnt flesh. Then the officer spoke again:

"The boys we are taking will return within two years!
They're going to serve the fatherland, not betray it like these
men!" and he pointed at the smoking corpses. "When we return
for our quota you had better cooperate with us! You can see
what happens to those who help the subversives!"

Toribio turned pale as he slowly climbed into the military
truck. He could not understand why—unlike some of his
friends—he did not feel like crying. He felt, instead, as if there
were a hard stone in his chest and another one in the center
of his forehead . . . When all were on the truck, he saw the
sky. The last rays of the sun shining between the clouds, and
the Morning Star, Kukulkán, were the only things he could
retain in his memory . . . Toribio saw the candy vendor walk
quickly towards his house. He heard the clamor of people
who perhaps were retrieving the bodies of the dead, and then
the hustling of the soldiers, the orders and shouts from the
officers amidst the noise of the truck that headed off for the
detachment, raising clouds of smoke tinged white by the light
of the moon . . .

A shot was heard, then another and another . . . Toribio did not see how the community buried the dead and held council, nor did he find out how, inexplicably, after the army arrived and entered the village and burned those men, the body of the candy vendor turned up discarded in the patio of his house with two gunshot wounds in the chest and a coup de grace in the head.

went down to the coast for the first time when I was three. My parents took me with them. We went to a coffee *finca*. Upon arriving, I remember that my father grabbed me by the waist, lifted me from the floor of the truck, and lowered me to the ground, which was very hot; I felt the heat beneath my feet. I looked around. There was a green field with a large shack in the middle. We were to sleep there, they told us. As soon as my mother had gotten down from the truck with my little brother wrapped to her shoulder, we walked . . . During the following days I helped my mother pick coffee. I would cut beans that were low to the ground or I would place the basket on my head to carry a load out from the rows of plants . . . One day, as I was doing so, a plane passed overhead, and I was frightened because we felt a drizzle come down on us that was white and sticky. They told us that it was a poison against plant rot, and we kept picking coffee. And, for several days the plane kept passing overhead. And then my mother realized that my little brother was dead, that he had died on her back, most likely from the poison since he was purple all over. And then my mom forbade me to cry and she told my dad, who was out picking coffee in another area. And the two of them kept working as if nothing had happened, and I too, because if the foreman found out that my little brother had died he would have run all of us off, and we would be without work. So we gathered all the coffee we had picked that day and took it to be weighed so they would pay us, and then my father dug a hole in the earth behind the shack with his machete, and we placed my little brother there. We carefully covered the hole, my father smoothed out the dirt, and we went to sleep. My mother hugged me and told me that if I wanted to cry I could, but tears did not come. I just looked at her with her eyes fixed on the tin sheets of the roof, and at my father, who scratched his head and passed his fingers over the blade of his machete . . .

From the time I was a small child, I have been of my own mind, and that's why I refused to go down to the coast. I learned to weave and that's how I helped my family for a time. But while still very young I got involved with a group from Catholic Action. As I was the only woman involved in it, the other women of the village began to gossip about me, saying that I liked to be with men and things like that. I didn't care because I knew I wasn't doing anything wrong, and besides, I thought that the reason they didn't get involved was because they were afraid. And since I had my parents' permission, none of that bothered me. That's how I learned important things: I learned why it is there are rich and poor, why we must struggle, and that we women have the same rights as men, and for that reason we have the right to struggle also. It was there in the village that I heard many of these talks; and later, when I returned to my village, I told my friends everything in the Quiché language. About that time a priest came to the village accompanied by some young Indians and Ladinos. They taught us to read, and from them I learned to read and write and to use fertilizers before planting. They talked to us about human rights. And many people in the village began to open their eyes. We began to understand our situation, and that created conflicts for us with the shamans and the village elders, but there was nothing we could do about it. It was hard for us to believe anymore that our suffering—so much hunger, so much death and the lack of land—was due to the sins of our fathers for which they had been punished by the Spaniards, and that it would not be until the year two thousand that our lineages would be liberated. No, we now knew why there were rich and poor, and we knew what the rich—the ones who pay the army—do. We now knew that the remedy for our misfortunes was in our own hands . . .

And what happened was that the catechists, the leaders of Catholic Action, began to have more authority than the village elders, and little by little they took over the communal organization. The elders said that the catechists did not respect our ancestors, that the secrets of the lineages were going to be lost if there were no initiates to become shamans, that if no one wanted to learn the secrets we were all lost because we were going to end up with no knowledge. But since the catechists received money from the gringos, they talked only of "development projects," and since thanks to them schools were opened and water and electricity were introduced and many houses were built, everyone supported these young folks who also brought a lot of fertilizer for the people that had plots of land. The Ladino priests who were behind the Indian catechists allied the Catholic Action Movement with the Christian Democratic Party (PDC), and the worst thing was that the Ladinos of the village began to distrust the Indians. They said that we Indians were becoming arrogant, that we would become rich and then who would work their lands, and they began to talk about Communism and started to infiltrate the Catholic Action Movement with spies . . .

In 1972 the spies began to speak ill of us. I was the leader in my village, and in 1973 the governor called me and threatened me with jail if I kept talking about injustice, freedom, and poverty, which was what I talked about because it was what I had learned. "Blessed are the poor," he shouted at me, "for theirs is the Kingdom of Heaven!" Then, as the power of the Ladinos, that is, the Christian Democrats, the military commissioners, and the merchants of the village, undermined all our efforts, by the 1974 elections nothing functioned in my village, neither the cooperatives nor the schools nor any of the projects. It then occurred to us that we could save ourselves through the Christian Democratic Party, that one of us would run in the elections for mayor, and that through local power we would do things our way. As luck would have it, there was fraud in the elections and General Ríos Montt, who had won as a candidate of the PDC, was not allowed to become president. At that time we didn't know anything about General Ríos Montt . . . It turned out that a Ladino became mayor, and then repression came down upon us, and our friends began to turn up dead along the roads . . . Out of despair, we joined the Committee of Peasant Unity, the CUC, without knowing that by doing so we would end up getting involved with the Guerrilla army of the

Poor, the EGP. In the CUC no one talked of religion any longer. They talked only of exploitation, equality, better wages for the workers, and popular power. The CUC was created in 1974, when Catholic Action catechists joined with the Quichés in the north, and by 1976, when the earthquake struck us, all the people in Catholic Action were in the CUC. The CUC was an organization of young people, even children, and they formed propaganda, self-defense, intelligence, and other committees, with a network that included all the villages of the region. At that time the CUC was not yet connected with the guerrillas who were rumored to be in the area, in the mountains. It was a very popular group. The truth is that only the Ladinos of the village were against the CUC. Then, when the earthquake struck and it was as if our world had been turned upside down, the people of the CUC were the first to organize the aid that came from other countries, and that surprised just about everyone since we were used to seeing only what was right in front of our noses because of some ideas the catechists taught. What the CUC did after the earthquake made the elders and shamans happy, because they said the communal spirit was being recovered and that the ancestors were content and that the *nahual* spirits would once again watch over us Indians. The CUC was becoming more Indian than Ladino . . .

In 1977 the miners of Ixtahuacán made their famous march to the capital. The CUC joined them, and in all we were one hundred thousand people. Seeing the miners enter the capital with their helmets on after having covered two hundred fifty miles on foot frightened the Ladinos. But the mass of Indians that arrived behind them—sweating, with their eyes flashing, their machetes in hand, in their multicolored traditional clothing, traversing the streets of the capital, stomping their sandals—scared them even more. There were students who shouted all along Bolivar Avenue. Others fearfully watched us pass by. Many people grabbed their children and carried them away, taking them home. And the group of Indians marching behind the miners (who were also Indians but instead of traditional clothing they walked along with their helmets on—the kind with the light in front—and in their work pants), wore costumes that frightened the Ladinos more: the women's necklaces, their silver earrings, *huipiles*, *cortes*, and sashes. We Indians never marched more forcefully than that time. I saw then that the Ladino is afraid of us and that what we have to do is unite. All of that motivated the CUC to participate in the May Day parade of 1978, and the Indians marched in their native clothing, walking proudly. That haughty gesture is what embitters the Ladinos, and we didn't really understand that that was a provocation to the Ladino spirit. For that, we would pay very dearly . . .

At that time many Indian *compañeros*, who were fleeing from confrontations between the guerrillas and the army, began to arrive in the village from the north of El Quiché. One of those Quiché Indians that came to live in my village was Don Vicente Menchú, who, like some from my village, had been a Catholic Action leader. Don Vicente had been imprisoned for his opposition to robbery of lands in his community, and the army captured one of his sons, a fourteen-year-old. They ripped out his fingernails, cut off his tongue, cut open the soles of his feet, and burned his body with lit cigarettes. Finally, one day they took him to the front of the village church along with other boys they held captive, and the officer in charge gave a grand speech and then he soaked all of them with gasoline and lit them on fire. Standing near the atrium, Don Vicente and his family saw everything. That's why Don Vicente left his village, to let Indians in other areas know about what was happening in his region and about what was coming for all of us. Don Vicente told us how the army arrived at night or in the morning, how the soldiers entered with their faces painted and burned and stole everything, how they locked the women in the church and raped them. And he told us that this was war, that in war we must organize ourselves, that if we didn't, the war would never end and the army would continue killing Indians. More people from my village joined the CUC thanks to Don Vicente's talks. Then he left, and we learned how he had died January 31, 1980, in the capital. He and other *compañeros* had occupied the Spanish Embassy to denounce what was happening in El Quiché, and then the security forces burned the building with white phosphorous, and almost all of them died there. One survived, but they took him out of the hospital, killed him, and dumped his body at the university. A Ladino *compañero* from Oriente told all this to an Indian from my village. They killed that Ladino *compañero* in Mita, and that became his nickname: Mita. He studied architecture, and he had helped Don Vicente and the other Indian *compañeros* organize the taking of the Spanish Embassy. They say everything was planned at the University of San Carlos, that they had left from there for the embassy without knowing they would all be burned to death. That's why the repression struck the university in 1980, and they say that there were seven hundred university people killed, among them students as well as professors and workers . . .

The first death in my village occurred that year, in 1980. It was in April. A man passing in front of the ruins of what had been the ancient capital of the Quiché Kingdom saw a man being killed; a masked Ladino was finishing him off. He did not realize that the victim was his cousin . . . In May they kidnapped Baltasar Toj Medrano, an announcer for Radio Quiché, and people found him the next day with his hands tied and his head crushed. In September, a death squad made up of some fifty masked men, Ladinos from Oriente, they say, arrived in my village. They pulled out lists of names and took those people from their houses, separating them from the rest of us. All of them were catechists, cooperativists, and people from the CUC. There were fifteen in all, and they killed all of them. They hanged my brother, who was with the CUC, between two trees. They stabbed him in the chest and mocked him for a long time. Then one of the masked men unrolled a nylon cord and slowly strangled him. My brother shuddered violently before dying, and the masked men just laughed and laughed . . . Then they began to search for weapons, even though they knew we had none, because if they had really suspected that we had any they would

have looked for them immediately. The only thing they found
were machetes. We later learned that the lists of accused people
had come from our own village and that the region's congres-
sional representative had been the one who had summoned the
death squads. At that time we had an Indian mayor, the first in
two hundred years, and a little more than two weeks later they
shot him dead with machine guns in front of his family. They
were the same Ladinos from Oriente that had massacred the
people from the village. After that, the Indians of the region
began to organize themselves in guerrilla bands to kill Ladinos.
In my village they were going to do the same, but one day the
army arrived and destroyed everything. They arrived before six
in the morning. There were one hundred and fifty of them.
Some were Indians from other regions, from other ethnic
groups that spoke other languages. Others were Ladinos, and
among them there was a foreign black officer. Shortly before
they arrived, some people from my village saw a jeep pass by in
front of the ruins of the ancient capital of the Quiché Kingdom.
A little later we heard shots, bursts of gunfire in the southern
part of the village. They were moving from house to house, and
before searching they machine gunned the families in their cots,
in their hammocks, on the ground—everyone, including the
children. All my sisters and my brother-in-law died there. One
of my nephews escaped because he remained lying beneath the
body of one of my sisters. He was only two months old. When
the soldiers left, we dug a large hole and quietly buried everyone, because if we had done a proper burial, as God wills, it
would have been a provocation. I remembered my little brother, poisoned by the planes on the coast . . . A few days later, the
people of the village discovered who had betrayed them with
the rumor that we were organizing guerrilla bands in the community. Council was held and the council ordered us women to
bring him to justice by killing him. So one Sunday we let him
enter the market as usual. Silently we slowly surrounded him,
and suddenly, without uttering a word, we clubbed him to
death. To distract the market authorities, another group of

women feigned a brawl, with shouts and all, and that is how the traitor met his end . . .

The village was in ruins because the soldiers had burned just about everything. So one day a group of about forty young men and women—all Indians—left for the mountains in the north to join the guerrillas. Later, some one thousand inhabitants of the village divided up into families and groups of families and, in the middle of a great rainstorm, quietly abandoned that place and headed for the mountains, not to join the guerrillas, but simply to survive some place far from the army. Men, women, children, and elders walked single file towards the mountains . . . I later found out that during the same period some one thousand Indians from the state capital had also fled to join the guerrillas in the north. Those that went with the guerrillas separated into groups, because in the region several fronts operated which later would be called the Ho Chi Minh Front, the Augusto César Sandino Front, and the Vicente Menchú Front. In 1981, the Ho Chi Minh Front blew up the government building at the very center of the state capital, and they also dynamited the roads leading to our town. That year and the following one, some thirty-five villages neighboring our own were attacked by the army, and the soldiers killed over four thousand Indians. At the end of 1982, more than ten percent of the Indian population had been massacred, and the survivors that fled from the army were more than a million . . .

I traveled around for some time from one place to another with my people, enduring sun and rain, planting a little something here and there, and then fleeing when the army approached. One day, when I woke up, I saw that we were surrounded by soldiers and that they were starting to close in around us. The people tried to run away, but several helicopters dropped grenades and some seventy-five of them died there. I escaped that time. That's how things were for us. Once we went down to a village for food, and we were on our way when we heard a helicopter in the sky. You feel a great hole in your stomach when you hear helicopters approaching. We ran to the woods and saw the aircraft descend almost to tree-top level. It was blue and white, and we could see an officer in his brown camouflage uniform, beret, and green sunglasses shouting with a megaphone in his hand. Then the troops emerged from the forest. Those of us who had fled when we heard the aircraft went deeper into the woods because we already knew what a massacre was, but the people of that village did not know, and they simply came out of their homes to greet the soldiers. As we ran we heard machine gun fire and shouts, and then we saw smoke rising towards the sky. A thousand people died there. We learned what happened a few days later from some *compañeros* from a guerrilla column we ran into in the forest. The *compañero* in charge also told us that the president's secretary of public relations (Ríos Montt was president now) had said: "Yes, we are killing Indians, because the insurgency has been able to recruit many collaborators that are Indians. Therefore, we have to kill Indians to fight the subversives. We are not killing innocent people but collaborators of the insurgency . . ." That's what they told us he had said . . .

And that's how we spent our time, crossing the mountain-side, evading the army the way a bullfighter dodges the bull. In those comings and goings I became aware that around my village Indian guerrillas who had been trained by the Ladino cadres of the EGP had organized themselves. They were always asking for food. Because we were organized and a family was in charge of our group, we were able to plant on several spots high in the mountains, where the army does not like to go, and sometimes we could give the *compañeros* corn or beans. Water was a problem for us—bathing and cleaning were a problem. During one of those encounters, the guerrillas gave us two old carbine rifles and twenty-two bullets. When we would run into them wandering around the mountains, the guerrillas would tell us about what they were doing. That's how I found out that they had brought to justice—executed—several Ladinos from the village because they were military commissioners, those who grab young Indians to force them into the military so that they

will later return to massacre their own people. And hearing all
this was wonderful because as an Indian I felt that the time had
finally arrived for someone to talk to us from our pain, and I
thought that it was possible for us to be respected and feared.
So one day I asked to join a column and I went off with them.
I did more walking than anything else, but soon they had me
setting mines along the roads, but I had such bad luck that one
mine exploded when a bus full of Indians was passing by there
and twelve died . . . I liked going down to the highway to stop
traffic and talk to the people traveling in their cars, to make
them pay a war tax. The *compañeros* ambushed army patrols as
often as three times a day. We would paint "Long Live The EGP"
every hundred yards on the asphalt . . . But later the army began
to knock down trees on each side of the highways and patrol
them in armed vehicles. Then we received orders to join our
column to other guerrilla ones because the *comandantes*—
whom the *compañeros* called strategic cadres—had decided to
attack the local military base. We were five hundred guerrillas,
and although we didn't take the base we caused a lot of dam-
age . . . In May 1982 we blew up three electric towers leaving
the whole state without power for four hours. The worst thing
about all this was that it always resulted in the death of many
innocent people: in the case of the towers two technicians died.
But we kept setting mines on the roads for the army, ambushing
patrols, and controlling the movements of the police. Time
passed and little by little I began to realize that we no longer
went down to the highway, that suddenly we would flee from
the enemy, and that we only went down to the villages to speak
with the people and to ask for food and not to organize their
support to carry out military actions. I noticed that the people
became more and more silent and said nothing when the *compas* held their meetings. That's when my disillusionment began,
but I still did not understand. I became truly sad when we left
a village once where they had not allowed us to spend the night.
The village's head man said that the army was going to come
and it was better for us guerrillas to leave. We were discussing

this when the daughter of that head man said we guerrillas were compromising them and it would be better for us not to return to the village—that is what she said. So we left. But I saw the first-in-command tell three *compas* something in secret and they headed off in another direction. Some Indian *compañeros* later told me that some masked guerrillas had killed the daughter of the head man. That saddened me. It disillusioned me, because the woman had nine children . . .

We continued roving around the mountainside, visiting villages. Where it was possible, we would organize a whole town so that it could defend itself in case the army arrived. We trained young men and placed lookouts throughout the settlements. We created escape routes to the forest and ravines and dug deep holes and placed pointed stakes in them and covered them with leaves so that the soldiers would fall into them. An important thing we always did was to help the villages after massacres. We buried the dead and cared for the wounded; we also took aside the little children that had been orphaned and played with them. Sometimes we even mounted resistance against the army when they were getting ready to wipe out a village. We shot at the helicopters and tried to get the soldiers to fall into the holes with stakes in them. We also organized the flight of people from their villages towards the mountains, and we told them where they could find others up there . . .

The massacres continued: communities were erased from the face of the earth. Animals and planted fields were destroyed. One day the *compas* decided that the EGP flag was to be flown in the territories under their control, and that's what was done. But in some villages people lowered it when they suspected the army might arrive. Sometimes the army arrives and doesn't attack; it passes by and greets the people, but if it sees that something is up, then it kills, burns, and wipes out everything. The *compas* began to execute people in the villages where the EGP flag was not raised, and they said that those that didn't raise the guerrilla flag were on the side of the army. I didn't like that because I saw that the *compas* were acting crazy, and I began to think about leaving but didn't know where I would go. In the political indoctrination meetings the *compas* always said that the army could only kill the civilian population in its counterinsurgency campaigns, but that it couldn't touch the guerrillas' military structure. And one would think perhaps that was exactly what the army wanted, because what use is a military structure if there are no people to sustain it . . .

Three or four of the founders of the CUC survived. One of them was Emeterio Toj Medrano, who worked as an announcer for Radio Quiché. They captured him. He confessed on television that he was a guerrilla, and then they say he escaped from the army and joined the guerrillas again. Who knows. All of this is very strange . . .

The truth is that at that time the guerrilla columns were no longer able to come down from the mountains because the army was everywhere. Although we were beneath the open sky, wrapped in clouds and birds and rain, we felt like prisoners up there. Sometimes only two of us would go down, but at the risk of being captured. More than once a guerrilla would get caught because a spy would betray him, or he would get nervous and the army would detect him. All the guerrilla positions had to be changed when someone who had gone down did not return at the indicated time. We would take refuge in caves and tunnels because a little while later planes would arrive to bomb and helicopters to drop fire bombs and fire machine guns into the forest. Besides, the military base spread out; the airstrip that had earlier been used by small planes to bring food to the settlers of Ixcán was now used by military planes and helicopters. The heavy army transport trucks that passed through the town cracked the asphalt, until the number of soldiers reached some twenty thousand . . .

We guerrillas could not even prevent the humiliation of us Indians, because for Columbus Day—the *Día de la Raza*—for example, the town's prettiest girls had to dress in ceremonial costumes that for us were sacred, and they had to dance in front of the base commander and his officers . . . In spite of everything, the guerrilla movement managed to maintain contact with the villages. We stayed away from the town, but often we would go down to the hamlets, avoiding the army, and when a patrol was weak we would ambush it. Perhaps that was why the army began the civil defense patrols, and the soldiers began to force men between the ages of thirteen and fifty to patrol twenty-four hours a day with other *compañeros* from the village, killing anyone they found along the roads later than six in the evening. When the army suspected someone of collaborating with us, they sent the patrol after him, and there was nothing they could do. They had to kill him and he had to let himself be killed because if they didn't, the army would kill every member of the patrol. That's how things stood . . . All of this that I'm talking about took place during 1981 and 1982, which was when General Ríos Montt began to give food to the people of villages that organized civil defense patrols. The military men called this operation "Beans and Bullets." And it was horrible. For example, you have the case of some of my cousins who died in a village in the south. The army was suspicious of five people there and sent the patrol from another village to eliminate them. The poor men arrived and didn't know what to do. They spoke to the village authorities and explained everything to them, that if they didn't do it, the army would come and everyone would be killed, themselves included. So they held council and prayed and thought about it for hours until they all came to a final decision. They directed the men of the patrol to kill the marked suspects; that was better for the community. And they all went to the cemetery and the condemned men dug their own graves and the executions were carried out while everyone cried. Five people died there, but in other villages there were twenty-five all told, and so on . . . The men of the patrols also have to kill their *compañeros* when they fail to show up for their weekly shift, and the worst thing is that they give the men of the patrols few and poor firearms, but they have no choice. They fear the *compas* because they have to kill them too. Around there one sees the men of the patrols walking along the highway, in the wheat fields or on top of the hills, with their old shotguns. Sometimes they are ten-year-old boys. And there is no choice; the guerrillas have to kill them too . . . One man, who was captured by some men from the patrols and escaped, told us that the men in charge of disappearing people have a special name and that they report to the G–2 on the military base. He said they are men from around here, although sometimes they are Ladinos from Oriente. They dress well and wear fine boots, but when they capture someone they cover their faces. "They took me," the man told us, "and they took my belongings too (I had a television set), and once we were at the military base they began to beat me. They were men in civilian clothing but they were from the G–2. And they are more important than the soldiers because they shout at them. They're officers. They blindfolded me and gave me electric shocks in one ear and told me that if I didn't sign a confession they had written they were going to apply the shocks to my genitals. And since I wouldn't give them a yes or a no, they applied shocks there and then I signed the confession with my eyes blindfolded . . . When they apply shocks there, your whole body shudders, and when you come to, you're sprawled out on the ground." That's what he told us . . .

So, everything was under their control, and what remained of the villages that had been attacked was left in the hands of the army, not the patrols. The patrols watched over the villages that had not yet been attacked. The patrol members were required to chose their own "Miss Patrol," and the girls had to compete in a pageant. When one was chosen all the men of the patrol marched and kissed the national flag and swore loyalty to it, and the flag was always carried by the military base commander. Our elders and shamans see that, and one realizes that sadness is finishing them off like the little candles in the church because that is not our tradition. The army is killing our traditions and is teaching the young men of the patrols other traditions. We don't know what their flag means nor do we care, but we do know that it stands for something good for the Ladinos . . . Lately they have been taking survivors from the devastated vil-

lages to what they call development poles, which are villages of
wood houses with tin roofs, all of them very neatly placed one
after the other, and everything is surrounded by barbed wire
with lookout posts at every corner. No one leaves there without
having their identification stamped, and no one enters without
that either . . .

But things got even worse for us guerrillas because we didn't
have anything to eat. And when we would run into people wandering through the mountains that didn't want to join the
columns, they denied us food, and then we had problems
because some of the *compas* wanted to force them to give us
food while others said no, that wasn't right, that they were the
ones we were fighting for, but then why didn't they give us food,
and so on. That was what life was like in the mountains: always
out in the open, rain or shine, cold at night and in the early
morning, the guerrillas just going around in circles evading the
army the way the bullfighter dodges the bull. And when we read
something that had arrived from the capital it was always the
same. The *comandantes* (or strategic cadres as the *compas* called
them, one living in Mexico, another in Havana, another in
Managua, who were going to return to the country when we tri-
umphed) said that the guerrillas' military structures were intact,
that the army's counterinsurgency offensive was failing since
only the civilian population was being massacred . . .

From the time the *compas* taught me to read, I spent my
time reading. I read a little book written by a priest whose name
was Bartolomé de las Casas, and I realized that these massacres
have been going on since the time known as the Conquest, and
that the Indians have been resisting any way they could since
then. And I have also read the *Popol Vuh*, although I have known
the stories it contains from the time I was little, because my
grandparents told them to me. But I have been reading that
book a lot in order to see if I find something in it that will help
me understand why we are all dying like flies, and the only
thing that is clear to me is that those in the army are *Xibalbá*.
That is the only thing that is clear to me, because they do not

want the Indian race to exist any longer. They don't want there to be Mayas: Quichés, Kackchiqueles, Kekchíes, Mames. They want to destroy us . . . I dream that Captain Tecún Umán must return to the earth and, even though it is not mentioned in the *Popul Vuh*, it seems to me that he is the one that speaks when the *compas* quote from the book and say: "Let everyone rise . . . Let no one remain behind the others!" And I think that we have now arisen. All of us. And they keep massacring us. And the *compas* are only worried about keeping their military structure intact, as if that structure did not also have to eat. I want to leave, flee, but I don't know where to go. Please don't tell that to the *compas* because they will kill me . . .

And that is the only thing that I have to say. That is all. What is clear is that *Xibalbá* revealed its face to us. It revealed itself to us Quiché Indians when the repression came here, to this place called Quiché . . .

also am from this place called Quiché, and here in these lands my people and I have lived happily since the times of our ancestors. But, from the time I was very young, we have been running out of land. They say that the army's generals needed lands in order to create their Northern Transversal Strip (FTN), as they called it. Father José, our parish priest for many years, wanted to form cooperatives but every time we tried to create one we ran into the problem of the lack of lands. Studying the Bible we had come to realize that God made the Earth for the enjoyment of man, and not so his rich brothers could take it away from him. It was 1969; it had not even occurred to us to organize in order to fight for land. Then Father José got the idea of asking the government for fallow lands so that we could settle them and establish a village in the jungle. We were all very happy with the idea, and Father José took care of the paperwork at the National Institute of Agrarian Transformation—the INTA. By January 1970 we had already chosen one hundred and fifty families from among the poorest to go as settlers, and the INTA had assigned us an area in the Zona Reina in Ixcán. We wanted to go to Petén but the INTA convinced us that it would be better for us to settle in the north of El Quiché. So we chose forty volunteers and headed towards the jungle. The trip took a week. On the way we ran into a community of Kekchí brothers that had settled there at the turn of the century. There were seven families. They cleared the jungle near a source of water and planted, but since after two or three harvests the earth would dry up on them, they would move on to another place. In this manner they had gone from one place to another in the jungle, and that's how they had survived and maintained their traditions . . .

We stayed with the Kekchíes for a while to use their community as a base from which to explore the jungle and to choose the site where we were to live. One day we crossed the Río Verde and selected the place. We spent the following five months opening roads and clearing the jungle with hatchets and machetes; then our group returned to the mountains of the

Altiplano and another group of forty took our place. Then we, the members of the first group, went down to the coast to work to get some money together to buy tools and implements that we were going to need in the settlement . . .

When all of us were finally there together, things became difficult because people began to fall ill. No one was used to the jungle climate, so humid, with so many kinds of flying insects that spread diseases. This situation went on for two years. But within those two years the community was already producing enough corn for everyone. What hurt us was the humidity. Wood did not dry out, so we couldn't light the hearth. Kindling took months to dry out and sometimes rotted, and it was hard for us to get enough firewood. But that didn't break our spirit. We had set aside land to try different plants, and we planted beans, melons, and potatoes, and also coffee, cardamom, and other things. Cardamom and chile grew best. There were one hundred and sixteen families in all, and each family group was assigned thirty *hectares* to cultivate and one to live on. The houses were situated around the civic center, which was the area that included the school, the church, the cooperative, the social center, and the Sunday marketplace. We also built a soccer field and a landing strip, because some years later a gringo organization provided us with a small, fully-equipped plane and a volunteer pilot, and the day arrived when there was a daily flight between our village and the state capital . . .

So we received help from other gringo organizations, and there was one group that even gave a cow to each family. Eventually the day came when I had thirty-five head of cattle. We stressed education and studied economy, sociology, the situation of women, and many other subjects . . . Through Father José we were able to get people to come teach us about our rights, because we knew that the oil companies were going around taking land away from people throughout the north of the country. We, however, kept prospering. We were even able to create the Association of Cooperatives of Ixcán, something that the government opposed because they said it would be a breeding ground for guerrillas . . . At that time we were paid five hundred *quetzales* for each *quintal* of cardamom. This was in 1979. In 1980 we had our first big setback. It so happened that Petromaya, a gringo oil company, carried out explorations in lands that belonged to our cooperatives, and they destroyed planted fields and ruined our harvests. When we peasants protested against these abuses, Petromaya threatened to call in the army. We were well organized, and we began to fight for our demands—the first struggle we engaged in. And it turned out that the lands we held showed up registered in the company's name. So we quickly filed suit against the company, and the courts made them pay five years of production for the destroyed fields. That's when the threats began, the kidnappings at night, and the slayings along the roads . . .

The cooperatives were the center of our existence. Even family problems were resolved by the cooperative. Justice was meted out by the cooperative. The cooperative did everything. Although as early as 1976 a female school teacher and eight of her *compañeros*—all of them communal leaders—had been killed, and also a Mary Knoll priest, the definitive blow to our settlement came in 1980 when they killed Pancho, who, whether he was operating the radio or making flights himself to take our sick people out and bring in food, was our connection with the *Altiplano*. When he died we lost contact with the commercial centers and remained isolated and alone . . .

By 1981, the guerrillas frequently occupied the villages of Ixcán. They would come and go, and the people gave them food and listened to their speeches, in which they spoke of the ideals of equality and freedom for all, claiming that the time had arrived for the Indians to free themselves. They had many Indians of several ethnicities with them. And they spoke to us Quiché Indians in the Quiché language, and they told us that the men and women who wanted to join the guerrilla movement could do so, but that we could also help them by providing them food and serving as contacts and couriers and in other ways. Unfortunately, some journalists from Mexico arrived in Ixcán and took some photos of Indian *compañeros* dressed in guerrilla uniforms, and they published a story saying that the guerrilla movement was made up of Indians. The magazine, called *¡Por esto!,* described how the EGP was operating in Ixcán. Then the army began to arrive in Ixcán, burning villages and massacring people. It was the thirteenth of February 1982 when the army came to our village. At exactly four in the afternoon we heard bombs fall and all the people ran to take refuge in the jungle. At six in the afternoon the troops entered. The village was abandoned; the soldiers found only empty buildings. The houses were empty, the school was empty, the curate was empty, the clinic and the church were empty—they found everything abandoned. And everything—the church, the social center, the school, the machinery, the electric generator, the safe with twelve thousand *quetzales* in cash, all the equipment and implements we had accumulated in eleven years of work— everything had been abandoned. The army spent the night there, and the people of the village hid in the forest and watched everything. The army spent the next five days sacking the village; they took everything. The people heard the shots when the soldiers slaughtered the cooperative's livestock to eat them. On the eighteenth of February the army finished sacking everything and then began to burn the village and kill all our domesticated animals: dogs, chickens, and pigs. It took them three days to burn all the buildings, houses, the school, the clinic, and the church. Then the people decided that they had to get out of there because there was nothing left, and if we stayed the army was going to come and burn all of us. And that's why the families split up. Parents went one way, children another, husbands one way, wives with their little ones another, and so on. Some families continued to live in the jungle, avoiding the army and planting in high areas where the army did not climb. Others, like Father José, for example, went to the capital or to other regions. Of the families that chose to stay in the jungle, exposed to the cold, the heat of the sun, and the rain, thirty decided to turn themselves in to the army when an amnesty was announced. The people were malnourished. Almost all the new-born children died; there was not one that was healthy. So those people turned themselves in, and the army took them to the base at Playa Grande and kept all of them there for a year. They severely tortured nine of them. Some died there, and then the army ordered those that had survived to return to the burned village. Now they are known as "the old-timers," because "the new ones" are people that the army itself brought to the village to rebuild it. But the truth is that the majority of the people that had lived in the village are in Mexico, near our border, in refugee camps. And at the beginning, the first year following the burning of the village, the majority of the settlers resisted in the jungle, but the conditions were so awful we decided it would be better to cross the border. I was among those that crossed. A small group remained in the jungle, and now they are known as the Communities of Population in Resistance, and sometimes they are confused with the guerrillas . . .

Life in the refugee camps was not easy, but some of us have had the good fortune to live with other Mayas who, although they speak different languages, are Mayas just like us, Indians from other Maya groups, and we more or less understand each others' languages. So we are doing alright here. We're better off than if we had stayed in the burned village because an old man who returned there as one of the "old-timers" tells that *"in 1983, after one year had passed since we had turned ourselves in to the army, after they had tortured us severely at the military base, the army took us to the village. It made us sad to see all that. We all felt anguish when we filed towards the center of what had been our home, our houses. Everything was black, completely burned to ashes; everything was tinged black amidst the jungle. Only the vines that were now devouring the area of the civic center and the foundation of the curate were green. It took the people eleven years to build everything, but it took the army only three days to destroy it all. But, what could we do: there we were again and we had escaped death. Yes the village was destroyed; they had killed it completely. It was ashes, a black stain in the forest, charred wood with little drops of shiny water—*

that was all that remained. The first thing the army did was organize us in civil defense patrols. They divided us into groups and assigned days and hours for each group to patrol. We had one obligation: kill every guerrilla we ran into. Or the army would kill all of us. And many of us did not even know what a subversive was. All told, that's how we spent our time, patrolling and rebuilding the small houses. But the army wouldn't let us build the houses where they had been before, because they said that if we did, the soldiers wouldn't be able to control who came and went, and once again we would begin to help the subversives. So they made us build shacks in the center of the village, the little houses one on top of the other like wrinkles, and we ended up close together. And when we would ask the soldiers if we could return to our plots of land, they got angry and told us not to ask them again. They gave us, the 'old-timers,' the plots of the dead and the refugees, the 'new ones' received new plots. Who knows why the army does these things. People came from other regions also, people who spoke other languages, but all of them were Indians. That's how little by little we have been getting along. We, the 'old-timers,' would like the refugees to return so that we could once again be a community, a hand with many fingers, a single body with one head that thinks for everyone. But we don't know what to do. We are like prisoners, one on top of the other almost, and with these shacks piled one on top of the other we cannot raise animals. Ah, but the government talks of nothing but these 'development poles,' as they call them. Just look what this man from the army's public relations office says in this copy of the Prensa Libre: *'These Development Poles constitute areas that offer the best possibilities to the* campesino *families. They have housing, technology, electricity, drinking water, and other resources needed for living.' Can you believe it? Everything that man says is exactly what we don't have. Now each settler is on his own. Before, the whole community used to meet every Monday and confer. Everyone spoke his Word, and the group decided what was to be done. Now everyone has to look out for his own rights. Hopefully, with this gentleman President Cerezo things can be turned around, because a few more years of this and we will not be able to survive. Because even though the sixty soldiers that were assigned to this area no longer live with us, they do pass by here at least once a week at the most unexpected times. The army is omnipotent: it is Xibalbá. It is killing the Indians around here worse than the Spanish did five hundred years ago, much worse, and no one speaks up for us. We are alone. No one looks after us, because the guerrillas flee to the mountains and don't protect us as they had sworn they would. That's why we no longer want to have anything to do with Ladinos, because they are all alike, big-mouths and liars, and they only look after their own interests. We are alone in Xibalbá and we have to come up with some trick to get out of here, to deceive them, the soldiers. We have to learn to be deceitful like them, to lie like them, to say one thing and do another. Perhaps that's the only way we can leave Xibalbá, with deceit, with tricks, by being clever like Hunahpú and Ixbalanqué when they were also in Xibalbá and played with the Lords of Darkness. That's the way we must play, alone, without Ladinos and against the Ladinos. That's what my Word says to the Face of the Sky, to the Face of the Earth. The morality of the Lord of Quiché and the Lord of Rabinal do not work with the Lords of Xibalbá; they only work among the wisest Indians, the brujos, but not with the Ladinos and even less with the army, with the soldiers. For that reason we should learn the ways of the Ladino as does our Lord Maximón, who disguises himself as a Ladino and a soldier but remains an Indian. We must disguise our Word as Ladino word, our Thought as Ladino thought, our Deeds as Ladino deeds. Xibalbá requires trickery, it requires deceit,"* the old man said, and it is true, because I have known that the army suddenly warns the village that subversives move about in the area. They make the men of the patrol go out and look for them, and they have to go because if they don't the army will kill them. We all live together but not in a community. They have taken the will to live, the desire to live from the people, because they have killed their elders and their children and have raped their women. The ethnic groups, the towns, they are mixed together, and maybe that is good in the long run, so that in this way all of us Indians will come to understand each other. We will learn the languages of the others and be able to start building larger communities, who

knows . . . The truth is they have changed our lives forever
because we can never be the same, neither the "new ones" nor
the "old-timers," nor those of us who left as refugees nor the dis-
placed ones that went to the capital and wander around selling
mirrors, knives, watches, and key chains or work as maids,
learning the Ladino's trickery there, in Central Park, on
Sundays, putting on high-heels and Ladino clothing, whoring
with the soldiers who leave the barracks to spend their Sundays.
Now we know where we stand, and nobody pulls the wool over
our eyes anymore—no one, neither Ladino nor Ladinized
Indian—because everything is to be found in the Lord's vine-
yard, as they say, and it's true. And evangelical pastors have
showed up around here—Indian ones, that is—that live like
rich men and give their children cars and send them to bilingual
schools, not so they can learn our languages but rather German,
Swedish, and French, and those children go around the streets
of the city already thinking they are Ladinos simply because
they have money. And all kinds of Indian organizations have
sprung up, especially now with that business about the
Quincentennial. Corrupt Indians are ripping off foreigners saying that it is to help us, the poor people. Sure. Those Indians are
just like *Xibalbá. Xibalbá* also has its Indian side. And it's not me
that says so—do you know who says it? The young people, all
those children who became orphans and who now are growing
up here in Mexico, there in the village, in Miami, in Houston, in
Sweden, in all of those places where they have ended up supposedly adopted, and also in the development poles. They are
the ones who are thinking this way. They are the poor, of course,
and they would like to fight, yes, but now they don't want to
take orders from anybody, neither soldier nor guerrilla, neither
Ladino nor corrupt Indian. Particularly now, when the evangelical churches are destroying our traditions . . .

The truth is the army wants to wipe us out, our culture, the
secrets of the lineages kept by the *brujos,* and the guerrillas use
us as cannon fodder, just as the army uses the patrolmen and

the soldiers. Only the guerrillas have another way of speaking: they say that they are going to liberate us so that we will be equals. But when the army comes they head for the hills and worry about their military structure. And then they say that things are going well, that only the civilian population has been massacred, and their bosses and their errand boys travel around the world asking for money they say is for solidarity but is really to help maintain their military structure. What good does their military structure do them, I say, without people to maintain it? The same is true for their strategic cadres, as they call them, who live in Mexico . . .

Finally, we Indians have understood. If everything that has happened had not happened we would not understand. They had to kill us, burn us. We had to go down once again to *Xibalbá*—as it was written—in order to understand, and not until now do we begin our climb towards the Morning Star—as it was written. We have now completed five hundred years of purgatory. This has been hell, and now the only thing left to us is to climb, to climb towards Venus because we can no longer fall further down . . .

When I was a little girl I was very happy because I did not know about bad things . . . My parents forced me to work with men that plow the earth, and the men made me lead the oxen. I was entitled to three meals a day with seven spoonfuls of beans and four tortillas, and they paid me five *centavos*. What I didn't like was that when the oxen wouldn't follow me the men would hit me with the whip used to beat the oxen, and sometimes I cried and told my parents about it. So I no longer wanted to work with those men who were so harsh, but my parents' answer was always that if I didn't want to work then I wouldn't eat. I liked to work with other men who were not as harsh but who worked cheerfully like my dad. With them I was happy to earn my five *centavos* . . . Sometimes they would have me scare off the grackles and other animals that ate the corn, because when corn grows one has to take care of the field so that animals will not eat it. And there I was, throwing stones and shouting at birds, and since they don't call that work they only gave me four tortillas with beans and two *centavos*. They say that isn't work, but sometimes I got exhausted from so much shouting and chasing the birds away, and there were times when I fell asleep under the trees. There is a rule that the caretaker who falls asleep has to eat corn stalks. Then the owner of the field made me eat the leaf and chew it, and sometimes I would vomit because the tender stalks have a bitter taste. Besides, if you fall asleep you don't get paid and lose your next day's lunch. I complained a lot to my parents, and then my mom decided to teach me how to make *huipiles,* tablecloths, and napkins. And that also requires strength, because one is there kneeling, without being able to move, with the thread around one's body. And the thread is expensive. It takes about twenty days to make a *huipil,* and when we get to the plaza to sell it, Ladino people do not want to pay even what the thread cost, much less for the work it took to make it, for the hours one has spent sitting without moving. And for what? So that in the airport and in the stores in the capital they can sell them at high prices to the tourists who don't even barter; but on the other hand, oh how they barter with us. And it is one thing that we Indians like to barter, and another altogether that they don't want to pay even the cost of the thread. Because look: we sell a *huipil* for 8.99 *quetzales,* and to make a body-length one without embroidery, one spends 1.95 *quetzales* when the thread is cheap, because you need thirteen bundles at fifteen *centavos* each to make one, and thirteen times fifteen is 1.95. The embroidery thread is extra, and you buy a little at a time until you have a box and a half, which is eighteen spools. Each spool cost eighteen *centavos.* Multiplying eighteen by eighteen gives you 3.24, and adding both totals (1.95 plus 3.24) gives you 5.19. Completing a *huipil* in about twenty days, selling it for 8.00 and subtracting 5.19, leaves me with 2.81. And my labor? And the food I eat during those days? No wonder we do not prosper! This is the way my people live, those that weave. That's why I decided to make *petates* instead, and that's how I grew up. One buys two and half dozen palm branches. A dozen cost twelve *centavos* and a half dozen five. In all they cost twenty-five *centavos.* Getting up at five in the morning and working until seven at night, one can finish a *petate* four *varas* wide and six long. The merchants buy them at thirty-five, or at the most, forty *centavos.* How much did I earn in one day? Fifteen *centavos* . . .

That's why we decided to go to another village to buy watermelons and tomatoes to resell at the market. The other village was three hours walk away. We would leave the house at five in the morning and arrive there at eight. Then it took us three more hours to return. Since I was only eleven years old I couldn't carry very much, only twenty-five or thirty pounds. My mother could carry seventy-five and my father, with his *cacaxte,* eighty-five plus three small watermelons that we placed underneath the tomatoes so they wouldn't get smashed. The bad thing is that this business was only seasonal. So one day, when the season arrived to go work at *fincas* on the coast, my father decided that we would go there. And we left . . .

For the children, traveling in the truck was great fun; the movement of the truck was exciting. If the trip is at night, the children sleep, but if it is during the day, it turns out to be great fun for the children. The bad thing was that when we arrived at the *finca* the situation worsened because we had to start by clearing the land of vines and killing snakes and worms in order to have a place to sleep. When my father began working the next day, he picked four long furrows for the four of us, because we were four brothers and sisters. The foreman was always on our backs, making sure we didn't rest. Our parents had to help us gather the *quintal* of cotton, because if they didn't, we'd lose our right to a helping of six tortillas and three spoonfuls of beans. With our parents' help we did the work for a ration of food, but it was very little for the four of us, and we always ended up hungry . . .

When the harvest was over we returned to our home in the mountains, but we were all in bad shape: I had a fever, and my brother and father had diarrhea. The fact is that everything we had earned was spent on medicines, and we were left with only five *quetzales* to buy corn. "I thought I was going to be able to buy a *corte*," my mother said. "What can we do, dear?" my father replied to her. "We didn't earn enough." That's why we had to return to the coast the following year. My mother didn't go, but we went with Papa. My brothers and sisters and I were happy in the truck among all the fellow Indians. When we got there, we built our little hut and we had to dig a well. That well was the downfall of my brother Nito. Since we didn't have any water, we dug a well, but a well for five large groups of people! It was not possible. We would have had to dig more wells for the hundreds and hundreds of people that were there beneath the trees. And since there was no latrine, we all took care of our necessities in the same place, and it stank. Whenever it rained, within a few days the well water was the color of mud and took on a bad smell. But what could we do? Because of the great thirst one develops on the coast, we had to drink it.

My parents called my brother Juanito, and we called him Nito. After being on the coast for about three weeks, Nito already looked ill. He was white as a sheet, but when we asked him how he felt he only laughed and said he was fine. My other brothers and sisters were also pale; they didn't eat, only vomited. When the harvest was over, having saved forty *quetzales,* we returned to our home in the mountains, and my father began to look for medicines because Nito continued to get worse. Finally, one day Nito swelled up and died. He tried to get up, but he couldn't, and he cried and cried. He called me over so he could whisper something in my ear and I went over to him, but I couldn't understand anything. He wanted to say something, but he couldn't, so instead he turned to look at our mother who was holding him in her arms and she closed his eyelids. "He went to sleep," my mother said, but that wasn't true. He never woke up again. (I don't want to remember your life or your death Juanito, but others must know about it.) I plead that you not ask me questions about my brother. I will only say that he died when he was thirteen years old . . .

My mother had ten children: three of them died and seven of us are living. That's why she didn't return to the coast after that. But we did. We went back the next year. And that was the last time because it so happened that in one of the harvests my father was carrying one hundred and fifty pounds of cotton on his back and he started to climb the ladder of the truck. The foreman who was seated on top shouted at my father, "Hurry up, shitty Indian," and pushed him, and then my father slipped and all the weight he was carrying came crashing down upon him, and the poor man couldn't get up. We wanted to ask the foreman to help him but since we didn't speak Spanish we asked others to do it. They were finally able to help him, but his feet and back were broken. Even today my father is crippled, and it's my mother who does everything because he can't get around very well. Lately that has hurt him because since the army has required him to be a member of the Civil Defense patrol and he can't do it, the soldiers say that if the Indian doesn't want to be a patrolman it means that he is a Communist and for that reason must be killed. The patrols have to climb the mountains to look for guerrillas, and my father cannot run, especially on broken terrain. For that reason he falls behind the others and later returns home with his feet swollen and unable to bend over at the waist. And that is the story of the damned coast. That's what my father says when he thinks about it: the damned coast. And so it is that until we are completely broken, we keep going down to the cursed coast . . .

We Indians are hard workers. We are not lazy, as the Ladinos like to say we are. The thing is they don't pay us enough. And besides, they take our lands from us. Now it turns out that the military people have discovered there are valuable minerals in the communal Indian lands, minerals that foreigners pay dearly for. Now the generals show up around here with false property titles. And what about our titles? Aren't they worth anything? They are papers from the time of the Spanish invasion, and we have preserved them. They are old and faded, but that's not important because they are proof that the lands are ours. Even though the truth is that we no longer have any land to live on, much less plant corn on. The rich grow cotton, coffee, sugar cane, and bananas, and they have huge *fincas* just for the cattle to eat. The *fincas* of the rich grow larger, and they eat up our little parcels of land. They expand like water and climb mountains and overtake rivers and valleys, and we Indians wander around landless, roaming from one place to another. And an Indian without land is not an Indian because even birds that are free have their territory . . .

We start working by the age of six or seven and don't even think about going to school, since after all, how could we afford it; we can't live on air. This is what my father says to me: "I don't have any way to get the eight *centavos* for your notebook or the five for your pencil. We can't live on air." I have heard it said that in San Juan del Obispo there is a saint who lives on air, but who knows if that is true or not . . .

Because I am so curious and forward, I learned to read from the catechists. And I took my father to classes with me, and together we learned how to read. You should see how happy I am when I see my father sign his name. Like the catechists we are, we have learned to read the Bible for ourselves. We realized that there are thousands of letters in the Bible, but we also know that almost all of them are the same. My friend Narcisa, may she rest in peace, learned to read the Bible a little later. She died because the soldiers did her the favor of raping her, and then they set her on fire. But, thanks to the parish and with the help of God, she learned to read. We Indians are not stupid, it's just that the rich know that if they allow us to study, very soon we will open our eyes and understand how much they exploit us. That's why they say we are stupid and it's not worth spending money to teach us Indians anything. And that's why we are poor. It's not our fault that when tourists arrive we are all dirty, covered with filth from working so hard, and our children are malnourished. The rich people and the soldiers are ashamed of us Indians. They say we are a disgrace to Guatemala, especially when tourists come. But that's not why they drop bombs on our villages; it's because now many Indians are guerrillas, and whoever gets involved in war, I say, knows what he's getting into. What I'm against is all the killing of innocent people who aren't with the army or the guerrillas. And I ask, if they kill all the Indians, who will work the lands of the rich?

I became a catechist, because it gave me great satisfaction and peace for my spirit. Being a catechist means going to villages and talking to the people about God. People like that, and it's a great consolation to them. We also teach songs, and the people like that too. They like to sing, because they breathe deeply and get the pain out. In 1970 and in 1972 some good priests arrived in the communities to tell us about God. They weren't like the earlier priests, who only talked to Ladinos. No, these priests came to our communities to convert us. But it turned out that they were the ones who were converted, because they saw our dried-up lands and the conditions in

which people lived. And they lived with us, and together we
rejoiced and together we lamented. We were all undernour-
ished. But what could we do? They were only a few priests. So
they decided to set up schools to prepare leaders for the communities so they could get corn and beans. And they called us
leaders catechists. And that's how we catechists went around
speaking the Word of God all over the place. Once I read a pas-
sage from the Bible where Jesus is tempted in the desert and
says: "It is not by bread alone that man lives, but by every word
that comes out of the mouth of God." But our stomachs growled
when we studied, and we all laughed at the sounds our stomachs made, how embarrassing . . . One afternoon we met to
study Genesis, and we began to read in Spanish. The people
protested and asked that everything be translated into their language. And that's why we started translating, so that finally
everyone could hear the Word in their own language, because
the people don't speak Spanish. We read that God brought
about Creation. He formed the Earth and made all forms come
forth, because he loved his children. "Who are his children?" the
people asked. "We are!" some shouted. "Then why didn't he
make us first?" "Because God isn't stupid. If he had made us first
we would not have had a place to put our feet and we would
have died of hunger. God made other things first, so that later
we could have use of them." "That's a good thing," one of them
said. "We enjoy the things that God left in our charge, right?"
The responses from the community rained down: "But if all we
have in our charge are our hoes and machetes . . ." "The only
thing I have use of are my pot and grinding stone . . ." A man
shouted: "I'm only in charge of my wife!" And there was even
one who said: "I'm in charge of my fleas." The people were jok-
ing, of course. So, wanting to put an end to it, I said: "Well, let's
stop here." But the community said: "No, we want to know who
has charge of the land." And I said: "I don't know," because I
didn't want to mix the Word of God with politics. But then the
community said: "The rich enjoy the land, they take it away
from us, and they don't even give us a little so we can use it the

way God wills." And that's how, as a result of learning the Word of God, the desire to organize to fight for our land arose. And when the nuns taught us about hygiene and nutrition, things got stirred up in the community, because those things did not make sense. They said: "There are three basic kinds of nourishment: proteins, vitamins, and carbohydrates. For children to be healthy, to have a good color and grow enough, they must have milk, meat, and eggs regularly." And we catechists repeated that too. Then the women would say: "There are no cows; a glass of milk cost twelve *centavos*. We have seven children. I make a *huipil* in eighteen days and they pay me eight *quetzales,* which are used to buy corn." And we said: "When children look pale it is because they lack vitamins; they must be given vegetables and herbs." And the women said: "But where do we plant them? There is no land for us to farm." And we said: "Children must be given pasta, noodles, rice, and bananas so they will be strong." And the women said: "We have no money. We learn but we cannot put into practice what we learn . . ."

Around that time the kidnappings and rapes began . . .

At first they just threatened the catechists. And if they didn't leave, they turned up dead. We can no longer pray or sing or say the rosary or the *novenario* of the Sacred Heart of Jesus. Ríos Montt's government annihilated many villages in Rabinal, and in each of those villages there were three, four, five hundred or more people. I know because I passed through many of those villages teaching the Word of God. Ríos Montt says he rules in the name of God, but then there is the case of my aunt, for example. The soldiers burned her house and everything she had, and when they left they told her: "If they ask you who burned your house down, tell them it was the guerrillas; if you tell them it was us, we will kill you, Indian whore." Jesus took the side of the poor, and Ríos Montt's government is killing us. It looks like they want to wipe us out. The army is *Xibalbá,* it is not the Heart of the Sky, or perhaps it is the dark side of the Heart of the Sky, which is *Xibalbá,* according to the way I see things and what the *brujos* say. In the end it is all the same. All I know is that God, the Heart of the Sky, loves me. If one seeks darkness one finds *Xibalbá* in one's own heart, that's why the soldiers are *Xibalbá*, because they are trained to glorify darkness. The most painful thing is that they are Indians like us, and their darkness becomes blacker. The Heart of the Sky also allows darkness to exist, that's why *Xibalbá* is part of the Heart of the Sky, but we can chose light also and . . .

The machete whistled as it cut through the air. Juan's face made a gesture of understanding and tenderness as it fell to his left shoulder; his eyelids opened and closed like a butterfly's wings as the volcanoes, clouds and sky spun around until, little by little, they faded and finally disappeared. Perhaps from the ground he saw his body take little steps backwards, like a baby, and sit down as a thick gush of purple blood sprouted from his neck, dividing into three streams—one bathed his shoulder, the other his chest, and the third the sky and then the ground—and the dried leaves and trampled bushes strewn about everywhere by the *kaibiles* with their machetes and torches in their hands, with their faces covered with soot around their eyes.

Toribio de León, *kaibil,* remained motionless for a moment looking at Juan's head on the ground. He then cleared it from his path before moving on. In front of him, a woman with a baby in her arms reached out an imploring hand before Toribio cut it off with one blow. When the woman shouted with terror, he yanked the child from her, took it by its feet, walked to a jagged cliff and smashed it three times against the rocks. The woman got up and ran towards Toribio, who was throwing the child's body far away. When he saw her coming, he pulled his machete upwards and one of her breasts flew through the air. The woman pursued him as he stepped backwards, then Toribio braced himself and, bringing the machete down with both hands, he cut her head open clear to her chin. She seemed electrified, and remained there, dead on the ground. Toribio pulled the machete out of her and advanced towards the houses that were starting to burn. People ran by him shouting, dismembered bodies writhed on the ground. He felt his blood boil. His hands forcefully squeezed his weapon. His whole body was agitated and about to explode.

Several children entered the forest dragging an elderly man. Toribio saw them and thought to himself, "They are the survivors, the ones who must tell others what has happened here," and he walked towards the burning houses. An officer had lined up three pregnant Indian women back to back. Holding hands, they watched the soldiers advance, they saw how they hacked up the pigs, dogs, chickens and children with their machetes. The officer addressed Toribio, shouting, "Proceed!" Toribio returned his machete to its sheath and pulled out his knife. He grabbed one of the women by her hair and threw her to the ground. He placed his boot on her neck and sliced her stomach open; a yellowish liquid gushed out. Then he pulled the fetus out, he showed it to the woman, who opened her mouth but could not shout, and then threw it far away. He wanted to grab another of the pregnant women but they took off towards the forest. The officer then fired a burst from his M-16 that cut the women down at the waist. They fell to their knees, grabbing their wombs. Toribio advanced slowly and was able to slice open their wombs effortlessly and throw the fetuses towards the burning huts. Three men watched this without being able to move. Five *kaibiles,* who had their guns aimed at them, then placed gasoline cans and torches in their hands so that they themselves set fire to the farm and poured gas on the motor used to grind corn and make *nixtamal.*

When the whole village was in flames and the stench of burning flesh saturated the smoke-filled air, the *kaibiles* made the three men finish off several of their relatives who were strewn about the ground missing arms, legs, eyes, noses, lips. And then the officer said to them, "This is what happens to those who help the subversives! Now go and tell everything to the people around here!" He remained lost in thought for a second and then suddenly continued, "But first, I want you—and he pointed to one of them—to pour gas on your brother!" and he pointed to another one. The first man refused with a firm movement of his head. Then the officer said, "Fine! Then you"—and he pointed to the third one—"pour gas on him!" The third man stepped up and, shaking, took the can and emptied it on the body of the second man. "Now set him on fire!" the officer ordered, pointing at the torch he had in his hand. Covering his eyes with one of his forearms, the third man threw the torch on the second one, who immediately burst into flames and ran aimlessly a few yards flailing his arms as if they were luminous wings until he fell to the ground and was still. "Get out of here!" "And you guys"—to his men—"finish burning everything and kill everything that is alive!"

The two men they let escape ran like zombies through the woods. They climbed a steep hill and stopped when they heard the anguished shouts of some children who came to meet them. They hugged them and continued their journey into the mountains. Each time they turned around to look back, in the distance they saw the smoke and light of the flames that illuminated the star-filled sky of early morning and made the sleeping forest crack with an uproar.

I t was the 15th of September of '81. By order of the mayor all of the town's marimba musicians were summoned to brighten up the Independence Day celebration. That's what they said. But that was a lie, because the truth was that on the 14th the marimbas musicians had played all night long, but on the 15th the soldiers came out of the woods and started to kill all the marimba players. They sprayed them with bullets, and this happened very early. And then the soldiers headed for the road to wait until the parents and their children showed up to hear the music and enjoy the festival, and there on the road they began to kill them too. The *kaibiles* cut open the people's chests with knives, and tore out their hearts and ate them. Because *kaibiles* eat human hearts, they eat livers also, and even kidneys, and they drink the blood of the dead and sometimes of the living. There's the example of my cousin who that day they hanged from a tree. They opened one of his veins and the *kaibiles* drank his blood from a glass, and yet he wouldn't die. He wouldn't die, and the *kaibiles* were savoring his blood. Later they took the corpses away in a truck. The soldiers had left so much death behind that the truck had to make several trips, and there were truckloads of dead they threw into the ravine. It was very sad to see that because all the dead were Indians. I defend the good Ladinos who couldn't do anything, but we also found out that the Ladino mayor was the one who had ordered that all of that be done. One poor man, who, even though he was a military commissioner, came out of his house when they were killing the marimba musicians and shouted at the soldiers, "I'm a commis . . . !" But he fell right there because the soldiers also sprayed him with bullets. He was an Indian.

The next day, some of the corpses they had left discarded in the patio of a house swelled up from being in the sun so long and began to stink. They were poor people. Three couples lived in the same hut and they had nine children. The little ones cried and screamed for days next to the corpses of their mothers and fathers, "Get up daddy, wake up!" the little ones said over and over again, but what could they do if they were already dead?

They were all bloated from so much sun. Later it rained, and the bodies were kept together and they stank. I went to town with a friend to get permission to bury the corpses, and some authorities returned with us, but when we got back to the village their relatives had opened a big hole to place their dead ones in. Then the authorities asked why they had done so, saying that the army was going to be angry because they had not asked for permission. The horrible stench made the authorities vomit, and they finally told us not to bury the dead people without authorization and they left. We buried the dead, but some remained along the road, and the vultures circled in the sky and no one felt like burying them. From then on we buried people at night, secretly, so as not to anger the army. That was in the time of Lucas García.

There were many more dead in our village. There was, for example, Grandma Andrea Osorio, whose only sin was to teach women about food and nutrition. Many women have been raped and killed for teaching those things. Grandma Andrea was an old woman, and the soldiers grabbed her in the chapel, hanged her from a tree, and opened her belly and pulled out her guts. The soldiers stood on them, and Grandma Andrea wouldn't die. When the soldiers left, Grandma Andrea's daughters went to take her down and bury her. And they buried her, but the next day the army men returned and killed her daughters also—there were two of them—as well as one of Grandma Andrea's sons and her husband, for burying her without permission.

In February of '82 the soldiers and some agents from the secret police came by calling the men of Pacaal, and they told them to bring their clubs and ropes. There they went, following the soldiers, until they arrived at the soccer field of the people of Panacal. And there they tied them up. And there they cut out Viviano Xitimul's tongue. And they gouged out the eyes of others. And they cut the ears off others, a piece of cheek, a finger, testicles. And, sprouting blood, they made them do exercises. They made them suffer the whole day, and under the sun they shouted at them, "Shitty Indians, lazy bums, damn stupid

Indians!" that's what the *kaibiles* said to the men. Then they took them to the lake, and their wives had to prepare food for the army. The soldiers laughed at the men thrown there, they shouted as they ate, "So we'll have more strength to fight communism . . ." After they had finished eating, the soldiers began to kick the men. They took turns kicking them, and many of them defecated on themselves from the pain. At around three in the afternoon they still wouldn't die, even though many of them had their brains hanging out, they wouldn't die. Then the soldiers opened a hole in the ground, and they partially buried the men who were still alive. At around five in the afternoon the soldiers left, and finally the men began to die from so many blows. In all, there were some seventy-two dead.

Another day we were all working in the village when the soldiers arrived and said to us, "Why are you sad? You Indians are happy; you Indians are happy people," that's what the army officers said to us, and they kept talking, "Go get your marimbas, observe your customs." And none of us in the village knew what to do, because the men of the army were capable of killing all of us, capable because that was why they wanted to gather us all together. And the officer said to us, "Celebrate the Word of God, bring your *tún* and your *chirimía*." And then we decided we would do what they said because if we didn't they would kill us anyway. So we went to get them, and we only played one song because the people began to cry. The army had us surrounded, and then the officer came out from among the *kaibiles*, and, raising his rifle, he said to us, "If the Indians behave well, they will have peace, but if they misbehave and help the subversives, then they will get this," and he raised his rifle. Then he climbed up onto the altar of our chapel and he kicked the Bibles that we had placed there on the altar. He grabbed a hymnal and saw that it said, "No/it is not enough to pray/many things are necessary/in order to have peace." Then he became very angry and shouted, "Now aren't they subversives! We're going to have to kill all the Indians, every one of them! And don't believe that there are no more people. There are a lot of people to take the place of the Indians!" Then the officer took out a small notebook where he had names of people written down and he began to call them. The unfortunate ones whose names had been called took off their hats and said, "Here . . ." And then a soldier ran to position himself behind them. They tied the hands of all of those whose names were called and led them off towards a ravine. The women cried and the children shouted to go with their fathers, and they ran to hug them but the soldiers kicked them and pushed them away. They shoved them away. When they arrived there with the men under some trees, they tied a noose around their necks and hanged them, and they left them there all day until night came and some of them did not die. The soldiers laughed, sitting there beneath the trees. Thirty-two died that day.

And I know nothing more. That's all that I have to say, Señor. Nothing more.

Rabinal. Four in the morning. Toribio de León, soldier, jumps out of bed and lines up with his fellow soldiers to take a cold shower. Through a little window in the bathroom, Toribio can see the star-filled sky and the Morning Star above the naked hills of Rabinal and the surrounding villages. He soaps up his head and exposes his face to the shower water, and the soap runs down his whole body. He opens his eyes and looks again at the stars and the Morning Star through the little window. He thinks that at that moment, there in his village, that same star— the Morning Star—must be shining on the blue huts, on the smoking roofs, on the greenish bell towers, and that the sacristan, Chalío, must be shaking off sleep in order to start the fire, prepare coffee, and climb the tower to announce five o'clock mass. But no. Chalío is dead, and Father Aníbal too . . . Toribio knows it. His memory knows it.

Sunday: market day. People come down the hills with baskets full of fruits, legumes, vegetables, animals, and herbs like *Sietemontes* and *Chilca* to frighten away evil spirits. For an instant, Toribio imagines bottle rockets exploding in the sky: *My dad must be making firecrackers and rockets up there . . .*

Since that afternoon when the army seized him in his village, he has had no news from his land. Toribio turned the shower off and, breathing the cold air, abandoned the small space for the next man. As he put on his uniform, tied his boots, and prepared his equipment, he thought, as his training manual indicated, that he was a *kaibil*. He would paint black stripes on his face with his fingers, and in formation he would shout with the others: "I am a *kaibil!*" And in response to the officer's question: "What do *kaibiles* eat?" he would respond: "Human flesh, human flesh!" "And what else?" "Guerrillas, subversive guerrillas!" Guerrilla flesh could not taste any worse than the raw chicken he had to chew and swallow during training in the *kaibil* course. However, once he was in formation with the troops with his face painted and his equipment on his back, he felt fear when he thought about the guerrillas. What were they like? Big, huge? Fierce, evil? *It was five in the morning at the*

Rabinal military detachment. It was five in the morning in the sur-rounding villages, and the people were starting to get up from their tapexcos *and their* petates. *They began to light stoves to heat water for coffee, because the commander of the detachment had ordered them, through the military commissioners, to go down to Rabinal again to sell their goods. They were to set up market again and bring joy to the town once more. Because ever since the army had come to Rabinal, the dead had begun to appear along the roads—coopera-tivists, catechists—and they appeared with their hands bound, strangled or with their throats slit, discarded there in the ditches. Then the people stopped going down to the town to sell their things because people almost always disappeared on Sundays. They disap-peared from the cantinas, from around the church, from the market's latrines. But now the commander had told them to please come to town, to bring life to Rabinal's market, and for that reason families prepared their baskets with* macuy *and* chiquiboy, *with chickens and small pigs, and with cheese and cottage cheese to exchange for corn. Other people went just to hear mass. They prepared everything and were drinking coffee when five o'clock arrived. They then began to head down to the town. The soldiers had hidden themselves in the woods along the path and watched the people pass by. Everyone was talking and laughing. And so, raising dust behind them, they took the turn in the path. When their voices could no longer be heard, the sol-diers walked towards the village. This was happening at the same time in all the villages of Rabinal: the soldiers let the people leave and gave them time to arrive in town and set themselves up in the plaza market. They then surrounded the villages and the officers ordered them to prepare their mortars. The firing started at seven in the' morning; the mortars spit out bombs. The people in the town's mar-ket heard the explosions over there and began to worry about their small children. A helicopter appeared circling in the air, and two small planes flew overhead as if protecting them. Bombs also fell from the helicopter, and the people saw this from the market and said: "And my children, and my grandparents, they can't run." "My chil-dren are eight and ten years old. Maybe they were able to take cover in the ravine." And then the people decided to return to their villages.*

But how could they, if when they arrived at the place known as Plan de Sánchez, where the roads to the villages fork, the army was there waiting for them? Some of those that were the last to arrive, upon seeing the check point, jumped into the ravines and were saved, but the majority of them remained there, at the crossroads . . .

Toribio de León, *kaibil,* with his face painted and his machete in hand, moved forward with his comrades towards the bombed village, through the burning huts, and started to seek out targets. The order: kill everything that moves, burn everything that will burn. This is how war is waged against subversion. Toribio saw his comrades break into the area of the village, he saw how an elderly man raised his arms in front of a *kaibil* and how the *kaibil* sank his machete between the man's neck and shoulder, how he put his boot on his chest to pull the bloodied blade out, and how, with the man on the ground, he cut off his arms and legs and left him discarded there trembling. The order: inflict mortal wounds, leave the subversives alive with no hope of surviving. Leave them to die by themselves, alone and slowly. Make sure there are witnesses and let them get away. Toribio saw how his comrades hacked with machetes the dogs that were tied up, the pigs in their pens, how they entered the huts and set them on fire. Five crying children emerged from a burning hut. The comrade at Toribio's side met them with a forceful machete thrust. Two of them, bathed in blood, fell. Then Toribio, sensing that his comrade was watching him, pursued the others. They went off in different directions and he could only strike one with his machete on the center of his head, which made a thud like a coconut. The child stopped in his tracks and shook. Toribio withdrew his machete. The child turned to look at him, then Toribio chopped his head off with one slice. He kept walking. The chickens flew above his shoulders and the blade of his machete whistled through the air splitting one of them in two. He ran. An old woman on the ground with one arm cut off tried to get up. Toribio delivered a machete blow to her waist, kneeling down to deliver it. The old woman grabbed her intestines which began to protrude through her multicolored dress, but she could not grab all of them and the brilliant mass began to spread out on the ground. Toribio continued to run. The machete whistles. It whistles; it cuts the air, it cuts heads that retain a fixed expression as they tenderly fall to one side—like the head of Juan—over the shoulders. He cuts arms and fingers and feet. He opens the wombs of pregnant women. He smashes babies against rocks. He cuts feet off with one blow. The order: humiliate the objective (the subversive *element*) and let others bear witness to that humiliation. The order: make the moment of death denigrating. The order: destroy religious and liturgical objects—images, silver croziers, ceremonial costumes. The order: kill the *cofrades,* the shamans, the *sajorines,* the *brujos,* the elders, the small children. The order: kill pregnant women, rip their children from their wombs and crush them in front of everyone. "What does a *kaibil* eat?" "Human flesh, human flesh!" "And what else?" "Guerrillas, subversive guerrillas!" Finally, over there, another pregnant woman. Slowly, grasping her stomach, she tries to flee down a cliff. She turns around to see Toribio; her face reveals the pains of childbirth. Behind Toribio a voice shouts, "Don't let her get away!" Toribio takes her by the arm. The *kaibil* behind him helps and between the two of them they drag her towards the center of the village. Two other *kaibiles,* who watch them arrive with the pregnant woman, understand the operation. The order: demonstrate that life is over for the Indians. They take her by her hands and feet and one of them cuts her belly open with his knife. The child moves, shakes, shouts, and is born. Then the *kaibil* who is holding him takes him by his feet and shakes him in the air and smashes him against the ground. The mother, with one hand on her womb, opens her mouth but no shout comes out. Then, the *kaibil* who has the battered baby sticks it back into its mother's belly. One more blow and her intestines pour out onto the ground. She takes her dead child, her intestines are of no concern to her. She takes the child and strokes it against her chest. The *kaibiles* shout, "I eat subversives, I eat subversives!" and they set fire to the last standing huts.

Only then Toribio realizes that he can barely breathe, that his
eyes are crying. It's the smoke, he says to himself, but he feels
like there is something stuck in his throat and also that an
immense hand is crushing his chest. He rubs it but it will not let
go of him. The order: kill the people that help the subversives
and watch out for the guerrilla columns because the insurgents
flee to the mountains when the army arrives and later they
ambush the troops. Then they return to the villages so that the
people will feed them. That is why the people must be eliminated, because they feed the subversives. *In the village they said
that Father Aníbal helped the subversives but my father told me that
was not true.* Toribio saw several of his comrades emerge from
large huts carrying silver necklaces, staffs like the ones used in
the place called the *Diezmo*, to dance the dance of *Tún* or
Rabinal Achí, and he said to himself that he never danced, he did
not even have a girlfriend. When he went to the capital on some
Sundays he always walked alone or with a male friend. Why
would he steal anything if he had no one to give anything
to. Then he heard the officer's order from behind his back,
"Withdraw, withdraw, withdraw!" And the troops returned once
again to the road. *By way of a secret route, on the other side of the
hills, the soldiers returned to their detachment without anyone seeing
them: they were covered with sweat and blood, some were frightened.*
Toribio thought his chest was going to explode. He arrived
trembling at the detachment just in time for breakfast. Next,
after another shower, the table would be served, the officer said.
In the shower, with soap running down his now calm chest,
Toribio looked at the blue sky of Rabinal and in the distance he
heard shots. They came from his comrades who had detained
the people at the crossroads.

*There, while they held the people at gun point, the soldiers
stripped the Indian women and raped them. One by one they mounted them, there beneath the trees, by the side of the road, while the
men watched. That's what the people said. They said that the babies
were left abandoned there on their shawls while their mothers were
raped. After these rapes—of some one hundred women—the sol-*

diers began to torture the men. They cut their faces, they castrated some of them, they cut off their toes with knives, and their shouts were heard even in the town. They then threw them all together there and some soldiers brought several cans of gasoline; they emptied them on the people and set them on fire. Two hundred and twenty-five people died there, and in the villages they left many alive, and there were also many who were able to jump into the ravine and survive. Miraculously, some of the dancers of the dance of Tún or Rabinal Achí saved themselves, and that's why the dancing continues from year to year, although the organizers of the dance sometimes don't want to take it to the street because they say it's too dangerous . . . All in all, that's the only thing that happened in Rabinal in the time of Ríos Montt. Nothing more . . .

Toribio was eating breakfast when he saw the second group of *kaibiles* enter; they too were covered with blood and sweat, filing into the showers before coming to eat. Toribio finished his coffee. After cleaning his teeth, he spent the rest of the morning watching the soccer game played by his comrades on the detachment soccer field. The pine trees whistled with the wind that carried their shouts far away. Beyond the naked hills that surrounded the town, the mountains were blue. The sky was clear, and although it was Sunday—he thought—not even the smoke of one bottle rocket stained it.

Toribio de León, *kaibil,* ex fireworks maker, wanders alone around the military detachment. It is Sunday afternoon, after the massacre. He still cannot think straight; he still cannot organize his thoughts. He is disturbed, overwhelmed. Finally, off in the distance a bottle rocket explodes against the blue sky of Rabinal. It echoes off every one of the naked hills, off each of the distant pine forests, in each of the innumerable valleys, and so on—Toribio thinks—until it reaches his village. He is a Cackchiquel; the Indians of Rabinal are Quichés—but they are Indians. The Lord of Rabinal conceded one wish to the Lord of Quiché, and he kept his word and returned to Rabinal to let himself be killed. What happened to that custom? What would his father think if he found out what he had done that morn-

ing? Pedro de Alvarado defeated the Indians in war because the Quichés were at war with other nations, and then those nations helped the Spaniards in their war to keep the Quichés from building an empire. Besides, Alvarado brought Tlaxcaltecans with him from Mexico, who were the ones who died together with those from here in Cuauhtimallán, The Land of the Trees, and those that killed the Lords of this land, The Lords Beneath the Trees. Division has been our misfortune. And the thing is that we Indians do not get along with one another. If we see in the Sunday market that an Indian is wearing clothing from another place and that he speaks another language, we don't even go near him. And we have to speak in Quiché, we Cackchiqueles and Tzutuhiles, in order to understand each other when we go over there to the blue lagoon of the blue lake of the Florid Place. The ways of the Lord of Quiché and the Lord of Rabinal were lost over time. It was the way of Kukulkán, *the Plumed Serpent, the Serpent Bird. It was the way of good and evil together, equal; neither was stronger than the other. Both could be practiced as long as it was done in a conscious manner. When the Christians came they wanted to impose only good, and it turned out that only evil was imposed. Good or Evil alone does not work. Each always brings about its opposite; that's why they have to go together. That's why San Simón and Maximón do good or evil, according to the circumstances. But that way got lost over time. Only the* brujos *can teach it to you. That's why the army kills the* brujos, *the shamans, the elders. So that the secret of the lineages will be lost. And the army kills children also so that there will be no one to whom it can be revealed. And they recruit the strong young boys into military service to Ladinize them so they will stop being Indians . . .*

Another bottle rocket stained the deep sky with white foam. Its explosion travels; it moves and awakens the volcanoes there in the distance. Toribio rubs his shaved head, bald like the hills of Rabinal where the Indians are suffering right now, with an arm, leg, or eye missing, with their intestines hanging out, the smashed children, the decapitated elders, the chickens, the pigs, the dogs shot full of bullets, the burned vegetable gardens and *milpas*. And he—Toribio de León—is sitting, watching the hills and the clouds, the white spots left by the bottle rockets . . . Alone he can do nothing—he thinks—and so he decides to continue doing what he is ordered as long as his military service lasts. He wants to be aware of what is happening, that is certain. He must do evil although he does not want to, but if he knows that he cannot prevent it—he thinks—he remains in the ways of *Kukulkán*.

The next day Toribio and his comrades are ordered to return to the destroyed village to help the victims, to cure the wounded, and to bury the dead, as well as to carry sacks of corn and beans to the survivors. They arrive in the village and many flee to take refuge in the forest. The officer speaks to all of them and says: "Do you see now. This is what the subversives bring you. Now the army is going to help you, we are going to cure your wounded and bury your dead. But if you collaborate with the subversives, the army will punish you too!" Toribio drags a sack of beans to the center of the village and helps lift wounded people to a truck so they can be taken to town. The ones who were hacked by machetes are dying; they cannot take one step. The officer orders the survivors to organize themselves in groups, in patrols: "You are going to go out searching for subversives," he tells them, "and where you find them, kill them. Above all do not let them come near the village." Suddenly an elderly man speaks to the officer, and he tells him that he is willing to be part of the patrol but that he cannot kill because it is against his religion. Then they carry him and his son away, to a turn in the road, and they hack them with machetes and hang them from a tree. Toribio, as he pulls the rope that raises the old man, hears him say before dying: "Thanks be to God that my son too has not stained his hands with a brother's blood." And he lifts his eyes desperately to the sky. Not even one bottle rocket to brighten the landscape; everything has the appearance of a horrible, inscrutable emptiness. Back in the village, the officer divides the groups and sets up shifts for the patrolmen. "We will return in a week," he tells them. "You'd better have a good report. We want results, the names of subversives. And whoever refuses to kill them knows that he's against the army." They unload more sacks of beans from the truck and drop them in the center of the village. They take away the wounded and the officer gives the troops orders to return to the military camp.

Toribio imagines his volcanoes as he walks back to the detachment. "What they want is to eliminate us," he thinks, but what can he do alone, he says again to himself. The column climbs a steep hill under the midday sun. In the north, rain clouds swirl around one another .·. .

he pictures embroidered on the huipiles *are taken from dreams, that is, from the dreams of the* brujos. *They are symbols from our ancestors, the ancient seers, the prophets of antiquity, and on the* huipil *they surround the woman's head because the center of the universe is consciousness and because the universe is a woman.*

That's why the men and women who weave embroider the world around the neck of the huipiles, *so that whoever wears one is surrounded by the wisdom of the ancestors, the intermediaries between the gods and man, those who control the order of things and the continuity of life in the world, and whose secret is known only by the* brujos. *Of course now, with everything that has happened, we have to make weavings for the foreigners, so we mix our symbols and colors at random and out of cloth we make little purses, jackets, belts, and even shoes the way the foreigners like them. What else can we do? It's the modern world, which has also fallen upon us Indians. The good thing is that there is money in this, although it goes to the rich Indians, who are just like the Ladinos. They are worse, because they mistreat the Indians who work for them. It's understandable that the Ladinos mistreat the Indians, but not that the Indians mistreat the Indians. That's why the weavings no longer make any sense at all.*

II
OTHER FRAGMENTS

N ow then, when a man finds a woman, he tells his father, and it
is the father's obligation to talk with the girl's parents. Her hand
is sought in marriage, and if she agrees, a date is set for ten or
fifteen days away, and the groom's family prepares two or three gal-
lons of aguardiente, some sodas and beer, one or two baskets of
bread, and a pound of ground coffee. This is done so that the groom's
family arrives at the girl's house and the wedding date is set. They
are married first in a civil ceremony and then by the church. Meat
tamales are prepared and then there is a dance with marimba music.
Then comes the ceremony. Copal is prepared in the groom's house as
well as the bride's, and the bride's father has to seek out two shamans
. . . The woman goes at night to the cimiento, where her placenta
was sown on the left side of the temascal the day of her
birth. Beforehand, a señora has dressed her and arranged her hair
while saying prayers. She pleads to God that the girl may have a
good life, good compadres, good health, and good children, and that
her man will not make her life bad. And the shamans burn the
copal. Then two authorities take the girl to the groom's house from
her cimiento after her placenta has been dug up in order to bury it
in the man's cimiento. The woman's cimiento then loses its impor-
tance, although with the arrival of the catechists, the women are
beginning to claim that their cimiento continues to be as important
as the men's, and this goes against our tradition . . . What happens
is that when the groom meets the bride they embrace, and the following day they have to eat breakfast on a petate, eating from the
same plate and drinking coffee from the same cup. Then, the two of
them address their fathers- and mothers-in-law as Dad and Mom,
and they respect them in this manner for the rest of their lives.

ong ago the people lived happily here. We didn't have anything, but the people lived peacefully. Until the people from Catholic Action came and made us see that there were things here that didn't favor us Indians, things like discrimination and injustice and all of that, because Christianity wants all to be equal. That's what they say . . . We knew nothing, and I noticed that when the men of my family began to talk about how we Indians were the equals of the Ladinos, that was when the repression started to come down upon us. That's why one cannot walk around anymore along the roads, because the men of the army come out and now they don't let you get together with others. We can no longer do anything, not even practice our traditions. Now you can't even live because the men from the army come around kidnapping and killing people. They wear masks, and disguised that way they kidnapped a man from around here and as they took him away they tortured him in front of his wife and children. That same day they also took away another man, and later they both turned up dead. Then the men from the army went also to the houses of that man's children, and there they left his four sons dead in front of their wives . . .

My family has also been affected by the repression, because the fifteenth of June they killed my father. He had gone to El Quiché, and how was I to know that they were going to kill him? That day, thinking that he was already on his way, I was returning home at around three o'clock when I saw a man's body discarded by the edge of the river, but it didn't occur to me that it was my father, and when I came close to him in the river—who can this man be, I thought—I saw that it was my father, but I still didn't think they had killed him, and when I got closer to him—when I could see—the dead man was my father! They had shot him in his ears, through his heart, in his back. He was discarded just like that in the river. Then I let out a scream, because why would I think that it was my dad? The thing is, the following day we buried him. But with great sorrow because we had lost our father. That very same day some people told us that the army was planning to kill everyone in my family, and then my brother went into hiding. We could no longer sleep peacefully, my brother was never at home, and we were very sad for my father. We were also sad because we were afraid when the people went around saying, "Now they're going to kill you," they would say.

Until one day, well, they arrived. The ones from the army. They showed up wearing masks, and since I had a brother-in-law, they went first to his house to look for him and my brother, and my mom said to them, "My son isn't here," she said to them. And then the ones from the army began to search the rooms, and when they saw that my brother really wasn't there, they began to fire their weapons inside the house, and they said that they were going to kill my sister-in-law. Then my mom shouted, "Please don't kill my daughter-in-law," my mother said to them, and the ones from the army left, but only to go kill my brother-in-law. A short while later people came to tell us that my brother-in-law was already dead. Some eight masked men entered—they say—and when they came in they spoke to my brother-in-law's father and they killed his son. They also beat my sister, who didn't want to let my brother-in-law leave, and that was when he said, "I am turning myself in," and right there they left him dead, the father of my brother-in-law as well, they left both of them dead there . . .

We didn't know what to do because they also killed one of my male cousins and another one, a female cousin also. So of course the repression has affected us some.

There are people who say, "Let's not get involved in anything," they say. "Let's just stay in our houses so the army won't kill us." But most people say it's useless to remain with our arms folded because in other places the army has burned the *milpas* and houses. "I believe," said a man who belongs to Catholic Action, "that we must keep on fighting." "But how?" said another. "We have to go to the mountains," said some. "What will it mean to struggle?" asked someone. Of course there are a lot of people who are frightened and don't know what to do. They don't want to know what is going on; they don't want to know things. Others keep working secretly with Catholic Action, trying to see reality for what it is; learning that there are things that are not in our, the Indians, interest . . .

Because, for example, the other day they grabbed a boy about eighteen years old. He was with his girlfriend and her mother, and, as they were leaving town, the ones from the army dragged him to the *milpa* and beat him all over. The women hit the ones from the army, but what could they do? They couldn't stop them, and they took the boy to the military detachment, which is about half a mile from the village. At that camp there are some deep pits filled with water where they throw people they capture, keeping them there for days and weeks, day and night, tied to posts in water and mud, in rain and sunshine, and they feed them one tortilla a day. But this boy was able to escape—who knows how—and when we found him we had to take him to the hospital because he was in very bad shape. Then the soldiers went and carried him out of the hospital and put him and other prisoners in a helicopter, and they say that one by one they threw them out when the helicopter was flying. That's how he died. He wasn't related to me. So my family has been somewhat affected by the repression that came here after the people from Catholic Action came to make us see that there are things that are not in our, the Indians, interest.

Perhaps a night shot of Lake Atitlán to start off will allow us to produce in the spectator the sensation of quietude. That's it, / some evening shots in December, a starlit sky, with the atmosphere cold and pristine, /several panoramic views from Panajachel towards the lake, / some from Santiago towards Panajachel, and / others from the heights of San Pedro Volcano towards the lake. That could work.

Then we can show / all of the scenery in the morning, at around ten o'clock, from Sololá. / With a zoom we'll start from the blue water and retreat to capture with the widest angle possible the town's steep streets, a mule hitched to a post, a drunk weaving along an alley, / and once again the lake; also some / rapid panoramic shots of San Juan La Laguna and San Pedro La Laguna, since after all that is where the action will be placed. I don't know whether it's worth showing right from the start some images of the army traversing the mountains, among pine forest and wheat fields, or if it would be better not to do that. Maybe a general aerial shot of some of the barracks at the Santiago Atitlán detachment; that might be very useful to help us show the contrast between the military activities and the life of the towns that border the lake. We mustn't forget that the little town of Santiago is very picturesque, with winding streets that rise and fall and people who go about dressed in their colorful apparel. It's not unusual to see an Indian woman, squatting, weaving a *huipil*, keeping an eye out to prevent the photographers from sneaking a picture of her. If that happens, she asks them for money, a dollar, even though at the time of our story it would have been only twenty-five *centavos*. Of course this whole introduction would have background music, perhaps marimba or *tún* and *chirimía* music—well, the latter when we are showing Santiago's church and its paintings. In the soundtrack we would have to stress that the communities surrounding Lake Atitlán have always been peaceful and that the violence in Guatemala in the late seventies and early eighties did not affect them very much. Tourism was their principal source of income, and there were rich Indians, very rich ones in Panajachel. The people of the communities of Atitlán, although dependent upon the peasant economy, frequently crossed the lake in order to sell their products and to buy consumer goods in Panajachel. I insist that showing the lake at night first and / then during the day will not only allow us to communicate the sense of quietude, but also—and this is very important if we are thinking of the U.S. public—to illustrate the point that this is "the most beautiful lake in the world." That tourist argument, along with the phrase "The country of Eternal Spring," according to the local slogan, ought to allow us to frame beautifully the brutal violence that we have to show. I know it's a case of staged contrast and that when we wrote the preliminary film script we realized the all-too-obvious switching back and forth between the serene scenery and the tremendous violence would bore the audience. I mean, showing tortured people, heads cut off with one blow, mutilated hands and feet, children with their stomachs cut open and mothers with their breasts cut off is what we tried to avoid when we chose this site and the particular violence that the gringo anthropologists documented here—a case of selective violence that lends itself very well to the elaboration of an interesting plot and an exotic and mysterious backdrop which can attract a wide international audience. That's why I think the contrast I'm talking about works perfectly, although we're not going to be—we shall try not to be sensationalists or propagandists and even less so, surrealists. Instead, we shall be "poetic." How does that sound? Although violent death may not appear to have much of a lyrical vein, I believe that biophilic excesses, like necrophilic ones, are orgasmic extremes which come together. Well, that's enough intellectualizing. I think there is agreement on this kind of opening, as it was laid out. Now we'll see how we can introduce the action . . .

I think the film should begin with the first kidnapping, because, besides this descriptive introduction we talked about, if we prescribe a chronologically narrated story, we'll put the audience to sleep. We can't stop to tell the story of how the military commissioners began to rise in rank and took control of the region. I think it would be best to show the first kidnapping and, starting from there, reconstruct the story. Look: Paco is sleeping next to his wife, or rather, both of them are getting ready to go to sleep; that's it: / both are getting ready to go to sleep and they are in bed. They talk; he can ask her if she put away the two thousand dollars the bank loaned him for the construction of the new church, and she responds yes with a smile on her face, / and she points to a small bag on a stool that can be covered with a altar cloth with the image of a saint or the Virgin. / The two of them are there in a warm and tender scene when suddenly knocks are heard at the door. / A surprised but calm look on both of their faces. / She shrugs her shoulders to say she does not have any idea who it could be at that hour. / He gets up and goes to open the door. / A half shot of the room, with Paco's back to the camera, might work so that when the door opens, the zoom will focus quickly on the masked faces of the men in military dress who capture him. / Then a general shot from the top of a nearby tree might show more soldiers hurriedly surrounding the house. / One of the last men to enter the residence asks Paco for his pistol. "I don't have a pistol," he responds, and then, after an order of silence, / more olive-green masked men enter the house and / start searching / everything / with abandon. / As Paco's wife gets out of bed and walks towards her children's room, / clothing, papers, food, and kitchen utensils fly through the air. I know that this is also very staged, as is the yellow spotlight in the center of the room moving from one side to the other, / swinging and illuminating, more and then less, less and then more of their faces, but we shouldn't forget that we must insure a wide audience and these concessions, I believe, must be made . . . / Finding nothing, the men approach the leader and wait for orders. / One of them has found the bag with two thousand dollars in it. / He opens it, and / out of desperation Paco offers the money to his captors if they will leave them alone. / The leader takes the bag, looks at the money it contains, closes it, and leaves ordering his men to bring the prisoner with them. / Paco's wife embraces their two children, / whose frightened, somnolent faces light up and darken with the swinging of the light hanging from the ceiling in the center of the room (a staged effect, I recognize and say again, but a necessary one). / Several men come out of the house. / Then the woman starts running after them. / Two stragglers are the last to leave. They carry off Paco's new pair of boots, a record player, clothes, eggs, bread, and meat. / They are all walking and disappear into the night. / The children catch up with their mother outside the house and the three of them remain there, / watching Paco and his captors in the silence and darkness. / Then the camera should show, with a general shot, the tranquil, starlit sky and the full moon reflected off a spot on the lake . . .

/ Men, silhouettes of men approach the camera along the road. There are many of them, and they bring with them someone against his will: a prisoner. The noise of a truck engine. / The vehicle rumbles down the road, / the men hide. / The vehicle passes in front of the camera and one of the men signals for it to halt. / He places himself in front of the headlights with his olive-green uniform. The driver brakes; / the assistant sticks his head out the window. / The camera, positioned at the top of a tree. / The distant voice of the leader is heard ordering the two of them to get out of the vehicle. / And there they remain, at the side of the road, as the soldiers climb into the truck, which heads off and disappears around a curve in the road behind a white cloud of dust . . .

/ Here we would need a quick fade-out, and I don't think it is necessary to show Paco's wife panting as she runs towards the municipal building shouting to the guards, telling them what has happened. We have to move to another sequence that must be planned very carefully, although I think we could prolong for a while the first one with a short silent narration of the death of the seamstress. Let's see: / the military commissioner, in native attire—known locally as "typical"—leads a group of soldiers at night to a woman's house. / She is sewing at her foot-operated machine. / Once again a spotlight hangs from the center of the roof and illuminates the scene, filling everything with shadows. They knock at the door; / she is startled, hearing the voice of the military commissioner ordering her to come out. / The seamstress escapes through a window at the rear of the house, / but the soldiers, who have the place surrounded, fire on her and she collapses headfirst with her back riddled with bullet holes. All of this should be projected without any sound, or perhaps with marimba music in the background. / A dotted subtitle should travel across the screen from right to left, which says simply **1980**. The faint noises of a telex printer or typing that simulates a word processor must be avoided. / While they shoot the seamstress, the subtitles should briefly tell, as in a cablegram, that Paco had cheered the ORPA guerrillas when they had taken the settlement and held a meeting. Also that the seamstress has attended a demonstration in Quiriguá celebrating the first anniversary of the Sandinista Revolution and that she collaborated with the radio station that the priests of the Catholic Mission of Oklahoma had installed in Santiago, which transmitted programs in the Maya language of the area . . .

/ A fade-in opening would be appropriate at this point, one showing a wide frame of the lake in the full morning light. That this is a regression—or flashback—should be indicated by brief subtitles that read: **1979**. / It is Christmas. The sky of Atitlán is clear, tarnished only by some torn clouds or the streak of a jet flying from one end of the world to the other. / Below, the Indians in their colorful dress. / Emphasize the raspberry reds from Sololá, the sky blues of Panajachel, the ocean blues of the setting, the cryptic designs of the clothes from Santiago . . .

/ A shot at nightfall in San Pedro La Laguna will show some carnival rides in the penumbra. Suddenly, the merry-go-rounds and the wheels of flying chairs and Ferris wheels turn on their lights as if they were opening their eyes. / A man engages the Ford motor of a merry-go-round, which starts to turn. / The camera now frames the rising and falling of the Ferris wheel. / From one of the chairs of the moving wheel, a group of people from San Pedro can be seen looking up at their children whose line of sight connects with theirs. / Three drunk policemen approach the scene: they argue, laugh, and embrace one another. Suddenly, one of them pulls his gun from its holster, and the others try to calm him down. The one with the pistol plays along with the others and waves his weapon in every direction. It goes off, / and the man who controls the merry-go-round's Ford motor is hit in the chest and collapses. / The group of San Pedrans get excited; they all look at one another with indignation. / As the crowd throngs around the three drunken policemen, the group of San Pedrans flee and blend into the multitude. / The camera, once again positioned in one of the rocking chairs of the Ferris wheel captures the scene rising and falling, rising and falling. Nothing but the noise of the Ford motor is heard. Everyone argues (in mute). The policemen carry off their comrade while gesturing "Nothing has happened here." / The faces of children on the Ferris wheel observe the scene with enormous eyes that slowly blend into the darkness of the screen . . .

/ The fade-in opens in the vicinity of the fair. Three drunken policemen stumble towards the camera. Behind them, a group of shadows approaches. The group of shadows attacks the three policemen; they beat one and the other two flee. Finally, the battered policeman is helped to his feet by the shadows and also runs off limping. / Faces of San Pedrans in the half-light of the moon. One of them is the kidnapped person from the initial sequence of the film, that is, Paco, the baker. / his face, his heavy breathing. Slowly over the harsh features of his face / a euphoric expression appears. He cheers (in mute) a guerrilla column that has taken the town and is holding a meeting in the plaza. He waves his handkerchief. / His hard face once again goes dark beneath the moon when the gathering in the plaza disappears as quickly as it had formed . . .

/ A military commissioner, Chofo, shouts at his henchmen, pounds the table with his fists. / Superimposed on his face, a shot of a bar scene. A man, his brother-in-law, shrieks at Chofo, who is having a drink at the other end of the counter; he shouts, pointing accusingly at Chofo. The latter then draws his pistol

and fires three shots into his brother-in-law's chest, / who falls
with open arms. / Chofo continues to shout at his subordinates,
giving instructions.

   Well, up to this point we're doing great. That's why I believe
that in a similar manner we can bring up that matter of how
military commissioners would order anyone killed for personal
reasons, and I give examples: the man who was kidnapped and
murdered for having married a woman who had been the wife
of one of them; and the individual who hit Chofo's brother in a
public brawl and for that reason was "disappeared" by the military commissioners' gang. In short, you understand what I'm
talking about. With silent fade-ins, we have to squeeze together this great quantity of information that otherwise might
overwhelm the U.S. public. What is really worth showing in
some detail is what happened to the military commissioners
who suddenly refused to participate in that business, and bring
up the case of the shopkeeper who, in order to put his conscience at rest, warned one or another of the victims that they
were going to be kidnapped. / Show three military commissioners inviting that man, the one with a heavy conscience, to
take a walk along the shore of the lake beneath the bright light
of a full moon. They smoke, walk, chat. / Upon arriving at a
small dock, one of the military commissioners draws his pistol
and, at point blank, shoots two bullets into the shopkeeper's
stomach. / Another one fires his carbine into the air, / and they
all go through the motions of pursuing a nonexistent guerrilla
who has supposedly killed the shopkeeper. / Illuminated by the
light of the moon, the people come out of their houses to see
what is going on. / Distrustful faces with expressions of
immense fear . . . / Perhaps an old, faded Coca-Cola sign on the
wall of an outhouse in the background can serve us here as a
humorous counterpoint. Then we can go on to successive shots
of the military commissioners talking with townspeople. They
tell them yes, your son, daughter or mother is on the military
detachment's blacklist for collaborating with the guerrillas, but
if you give some five or six hundred *quetzales* to bribe a few offi-

cials, they themselves will remove the names from the list. / Some refuse with indignation and disappear from the scene, / but a short while later they are knifed or machine-gunned down (in mute). / The military commissioners, drunk, head down a dusty road in a pickup truck. They terrify tourists; they rape women beneath the trees; in the thickets along the road they strip men and beat them. / The face of a merchant who delivers nine hundred *quetzales* so they will not kill his son. / Fade-ins of the boy ranting at the clique of military commissioners and of his kidnapping. / The pickup blocking his path, / men pouring out of the ditches, / a struggle with the boy, rifle-butt blows to his head. / They throw him in the truck and disappear leaving a cloud of smoke. / When he comes to, the boy is tied to a sack filled with sand / and is then thrown into the lake from the small dock shown in the previous sequence. / Continued fade-ins of the band arriving at houses where they take chickens, a goat, money, pigs, ducks, even a television set. / Twelve members of the gang now rape a woman on the shore of the lake: / her brilliant face, / her damp hair adheres to her forehead and cheeks, / the grass torn by her hand, broken breathing, the noises from the vegetation, moans.

/ Subtitles: **1981**. An army official arrives in San Pedro. / In an open town meeting, some brave San Pedrans request that the officer from the detachment remove the military commissioners and replace them with others. / The officer argues that San Pedro is a beehive of guerrilla activity and that, according to the military commissioners themselves, their numbers need to be increased and they all need to be armed. / Faces of distrustful San Pedrans. / Dissolve into a close up of a shipment of rifles, and then subtitles: **1982**. / A new dissolve of San Pedrans who speak and write a petition for withdrawal or replacement of the band of military commissioners. / The document is addressed to the President of the Republic, General Romeo Lucas García. / Subtitles: **March 23, 1982: General Efraín Ríos Montt's coup**. Archival photographs: tanks circling the National Palace in Guatemala City and troop movements in front of the Cathedral and the Portal del Comercio building. / Then go to a general shot of the military junta: Ríos Montt, Gordillo, Maldonado Schaad, and other officers behind them, all in military fatigues. / Ríos Montt speaks (in mute) over the television; he smiles, continues speaking, smiles again. His face is suddenly frozen on the screen, eyeballs bulging from their sockets, a cynical and anxious smile, a ridiculous mustache. The sequence slowly closes with a fade-out and the screen remains black for a long time . . .

/ Open with another fade-in to frame a large group of San Pedrans preparing a new petition, addressed this time to Ríos Montt, asking that the military commissioners be replaced. / Within its frame the camera favors Tono, the one selected to carry the document to the capital. / Tono's trip: a dilapidated bus climbing the tortuous highway that borders the lake. / The water sparkles intensely; the sky is calm; the volcanoes sleep in blue (*everything is blue in the concavity of the sky, in the blue hole of the Florid Place. Blue, blue dreaming. Only the Spirit of the Heart of the Sky seems to float over the blue waters . . .*) / Inside a bus: the floor is muddy, / *caites* and hands covered with dirt, calloused heels, hardened fingernails, red pants with black stripes, red *capixayes* with black arabesques, palm sombreros, / little pigs that squeal desperately, hens with idiotic eyes, chicks oblivious to the world, terrified iguanas, sweets melting in yellow leaf wrappings, colored *melcochita* candies pink and sky-blue in sleeping hands, / snot-nosed kids with tender mouths and dirty fingernails, the people from the towns that line the lake, / squirming bass tied at the mouth with reeds, / empty soda bottles spinning around on the floor of the noisy, cumbersome machine, / one or more transistor radios from which comes the voice of an announcer narrating with excessive enthusiasm a soccer game . . . / the face of Tono, / who is carrying the document wrapped in a plastic bag and who / looks at the lake through the dirty window, the crying of newborns / strapped to the backs of women with brightly colored shawls with flashy tassels. The bus moves away . . . further away . . . The camera allows it to creep along the mountain on a winding road that blends into the pine and oak trees until it disappears into the profound darkness of the screen . . .

/ Bureaucrats in the National Palace give explanations (in mute) to Tono and they inform him that the petition from the villagers of San Pedro will not succeed. / Tono sad, / Tono leaving the National Palace, / Tono in the Bus Station, / Tono, in a full zoom-in, surrounded by yellow flowers and vegetables and legumes and various fruits, / Tono seated on the return bus to San Pedro among Indians wearing clothes of every color. / Subtitles above Lake Atitlán: **June 15, 1982: the Mayor of San Pedro is removed from his position. He is replaced by Chinto, appointed personally by Ríos Montt himself**. The lake is calm, asleep in a blue, profane dream, enshrouded in very thick white clouds that embrace the blue volcanoes emerging from the water for centuries. *Only the spirit of the sky moves above the waters* . . . / Chinto paces proudly through town giving notice that he is now the mayor. He greets people, waiving his hand in the air; he rubs the pistol at his waist.

/ Flashback to 1956. Subtitles: **1956**. Chinto, very young, arrives at the capital to enlist in the army. A mambo is heard on the soundtrack: *the water jug is on the ground, and mama I can't lift it up . . . I just can't lift it up* . . . / Fade-in of Chinto in honor-guard garrison uniform, / then in presidential guard uniform, / then, with a civilian hat and in jacket and tie driving an automobile of the presidency of the republic / and, finally, as cook for the defense minister. / Superimposed, Chinto shooting at the seamstress; he smiles beneath the handkerchief covering his face . . . / Chinto walking along a street of San Pedro greeting people. / A group of San Pedrans observe him with caution. / He enters the town hall and / the guards come to attention as he passes . . .

/ Superimposition: Tono and his friends draw up telegrams to send to Ríos Montt denouncing the military commissioners and their atrocities. They draft petitions that Tono takes to a military base in the capital. He is turned away everywhere, except at the detachment closest by, where he is taken prisoner. / Tono's wife looking at the clock. When she verifies that her husband has not returned home on time, / she takes from beneath the mattress a telegram addressed to Ríos Montt and / runs to the telegraph office. The camera closes with a rapid fade-out . . .

Suspended in the morning, the blue lake reverberates. The motors of two military boats break the silence of the sky and the waves beat the water. From the Cerro de Oro naval base, several sailors have set off towards San Pedro La Laguna. / The boats speed steadily, crossing the lake in a straight line. / The sailors disembark and without further ado head towards the municipality. / The officer in charge enters. / Chinto, Chofo, and other military commissioners greet the officer and move to embrace him, but he, with a quick motion, tells his men to surround and apprehend them. / Surprise on the faces of the military commissioners; their nervous smiles—is this a joke, or could it be that General Ríos Montt has received reports from the town? / The people have come out of their houses and sheds, and they watch the sailors take away the military commissioners to the boats and then / cross the lake headed towards Cerro de Oro. / The question floats in the air, was it Tono's trips to the capital that had finally produced results? Or was it the telegraph that his wife sent? / People express their opinion. A woman says that she gave information to the detachment and that that's why they came to take the military commissioners away. She said they had threatened her and that they had asked her for money, so she herself took the money to them so they would remove her name from the rumored black list. An officer told her that her name was not on any list, and he asked her who had told her that. Only a few days passed from that moment to the capture of the military commissioners . . .

/ Cerro de Oro: browned by the sun, the small hill appears to observe the quickly passing military boats. The voice of Miguel Angel Asturias thunders from the soundtrack: *Boats with vendors of turpentine, medicinal leaves, and roots. Boats of chicken vendors. Boats of vendors of* maguey *rope, reeds for making mats, wood for slingshots,* ocote, *small and large pieces of earthenware,*

cured and uncured animal skins, cups and masks of clay. Boats of
vendors of macaws, parrots, coconuts, fresh resins, squash with very
fine seeds. The priests rose watching the volcano from the large pine
trees. Oracle of peace and of war, a cloud-covered volcano was a har-
binger of peace, of security in the Florid Place, and when there were
no clouds, it was an omen of war, of an enemy invasion. A cloudless
volcano meant war. / Superimposed over Cerro de Oro appears
the little volcano which serves as the logo for the Revolutionary
Organization of the People in Arms—ORPA. Its meaning: a
cloudless volcano equals war. / In mute, an ORPA meeting in
Santiago Atitlán: the guerrillas speak, gesture, / then march off
and never return . . .

/ The military commissioners being tortured in a jail cell: /
they confess everything they have done to the people from the
towns around the lake. / Bleeding and exhausted, the soldiers
return with them in boats to San Pedro and / take them from the
boats and display them to a gathering in the plaza. "These are
the guerrillas from around here!" an officer shouts. "They painted slogans on the walls and killed and extorted money! But
that's all over now! That's what the armed forces are for! Peace
has been restored to Atitlán!" A long silence. / A panoramic shot
of a thousand San Pedrans congregated in the central plaza. The
seven prisoners stare at the ground. Subtitles: **November 7,
1982**. Twenty soldiers guard the area between the crowd and
the prisoners. Suddenly, from a loudspeaker, the officer's voice
thunders again in the peaceful setting: "We soldiers are here to
preserve the peace! We're not here to kill or threaten people! In
order to prevent that, and so you can denounce any abuses, we
are creating the Civil Defense patrol in San Pedro and name a
new Chief of the military commissioners! These men," and he
points at the tortured men, "will be moved to the Sololá jail."

/ Subtitles: **1983**. A group of soldiers knocks at the door of
a house; / the military commissioner, who in the previous
sequence had filled the sack with sand to throw the boy in the
lake, comes to open the door, and an officer says to him: "So
we're filling sacks with sand, are we?" And the military com-

missioner exclaims: "No sir, Lieutenant, I—" But the officer interrupts him and orders: "Take him away!" / Superimposed on the screen, a copy of the request for a death sentence for the military commissioners drawn up by four of the townsmen. / It is carried to the National Palace of Guatemala to be delivered in person to Ríos Montt. / A medium shot should show four men leaving the National Palace and entering the *Prensa Libre* newspaper building with a copy of the notification. / Shots of newsprint and headlines from the newspaper. The April 12, 1983, edition of *Prensa Libre* should appear on the screen superimposed on the four men who deliver that notice. It should say that more than eight thousand San Pedrans ask that the military commissioners receive a death sentence and include a list of the crimes ascribed to them.

/ In turn, the ex-military commissioners draft a document in which they falsely accuse themselves of belonging to the guerrilla group known as the Revolutionary Movement of the People IXIM, in an attempt to qualify for the amnesty proclaimed by Ríos Montt.

/ Archival materials: Coup d'etat against Ríos Montt—dates and military movements. / The false accusation and petition for amnesty now appear to be directed to the new chief of state, General Oscar Mejía Víctores. / The denial appears as a front page headline superimposed over the general's image speaking on television (in mute). / A slow fade-in takes us to a medium shot of a certain Colonel Rébuli, who travels along the highway in a jeep escorted by two other vehicles. He is heading towards San Pedro La Laguna to take control of the military command of that region, and the subtitles indicate that the date is **November 15, 1983**.

/ The plaza of San Pedro: Colonel Rébuli removes the Mayor from his office at the petition of the community, he hands out beans and corn in the amount of one *quintal* of beans and five *quintales* of corn to each of the widows of the San Pedran men killed or disappeared, and he names Chencho the new head of the military commissioners.

/ In slow motion, the Colonel and his bodyguards driving in the outskirts of Cerro de Oro. / We should show in a traveling shot and at regular speed the ORPA guerrillas hiding, waiting for the vehicles to pass by. / The slow-motion shot shows how, all of a sudden, the Claymore mines explode and how the zones of fire prepared for the ambush fall on the colonel and his soldiers. / As the bullet-ridden colonel collapses against the blue backdrop of Cerro de Oro, behind his corpse in an instant eternalized by a still, subtitles display **November 20, 1983**. / Superimposed over the colonel's slow-motion fall, appears the ORPA communiqué in which this group takes responsibility for his death. The communiqué spins on the screen until it comes to a stop and is legible, then the camera slowly closes in a fade-out . . .

/ Background information on Chencho, the new head of the military commissioners: faithful to his Pentecostal Church of America, his community, his wife, and his three children. He works in the countryside. / In the distance, he is seen working the land, / then he appears convening the civil defense patrol and organizing shifts for its members. / From time to time he travels to Sololá to report to a lieutenant at the military base. / Chencho is climbing a steep street in Sololá, / then he walks along the highway to the base. / He enters and waits in an office for the Lieutenant's arrival. / He gives a report informing the officer that the members of the gang of ex-military commissioners who remained free tried to bribe him and then demanded he pay them three hundred dollars. He refused; he does not care if they kill him, he says.

/ Each member of the civil defense patrol donates five *centavos* for Chencho's trips to Sololá. They collect fifty *quetzales* each month, and Chencho is given seven *quetzales* each time he travels to give his report. / He informs the Lieutenant that he, as military commissioner, cannot denounce any San Pedran because his religion prohibits him from killing. / The Lieutenant tells him that he has received reports that Chencho is charging the civil defense patrol a tax. / Chencho denies it, saying it is a collection at the initiative of the community. Anyway, he will no longer accept money for his trips, he says.

/ Background information on Pedro, Chencho's uncle. He fights tirelessly to prevent the release of the detained ex-military commissioners: / He is shown signing documents and collecting signatures. He proposes the capture of ten additional men. / The sentences of the captive men appear in subtitles over the face of Uncle Pedro. Chinto receives twelve years in prison, Chofo ten, and the seven remaining men get four years each.

/ Subtitles: **The end of 1984 and the beginning of 1985**. Hearing rumors that the prisoners were going to be released, Chencho and his uncle Pedro quickly take steps against them and, at the same time, continue refusing to provide the army with names of alleged subversives in the town. All of this, by the way, is shown through another sequence of very quick juxtapositions and dissolves . . .

/ Nighttime. Outdoors. Thickets. The civil defense patrol disperses in the countryside. / A patrolman stands guard. He suddenly stands up. He sees something strange. A constable from the municipality—whom he knows—points out for two strangers the houses of the military commissioners. / Zoom close up on the strangers' faces: both are dark-skinned with mustaches, their chubby bodies suggesting that they are not soldiers. / In a quick superimposition, the same faces laugh. They are drinking in a San Pedro cantina. / Chencho, followed by the patrolman who had seen them the night before. / Chencho asks them who they are. They identify themselves as agents of the army investigating a matter that is no one's business. / Chencho, surrounded by collaborators, writes a memorandum in which he holds the municipality's constable responsible for the disappearance or death of any of the new military commissioners . . .

/ Another day: the sun extracting the volcano's blue light, the blue reverberation of the lake, the blue filter of the sky (*everything is blue in the concave form of the sky, on the surface of the Earth, in the sound of the water, in the waves on the blue lake in the blue hole of the Florid Place*). / Uncle Pedro at the dock of

Panajachel, with a sack over his shoulder, prepares to board a boat for town. He has come to shop. / He is detained by two hands on his shoulders. / It's the two individuals we already know, the ones who have seen the military commissioners' houses, the ones who have been drinking in town, the army agents. / "The Lieutenant wants to see you in Sololá immediately," one of them tells him. "We have orders to take you there, so please come with us." / Pedro's face falls apart. He turns to look towards his boat and is able to tell one of the passengers: "Please let my wife know they have taken me." They carry Pedro away holding him and watching him closely, speaking to him in his ear: / Pedro's resigned look crosses the entire wide-angle lens, which then remains fixed on the sky, in which there is a broken cloud in the shape of a clenched fist. / The camera begins to close with a slow fade-out / to rise to the star-filled night, the cold night with moonlight that illuminates the lifeless lake, several dead volcanoes, some dead hills, and a dead sky full of lights. / One of the passengers from the Panajachel boat informs Chencho of the kidnapping of his uncle Pedro. / Something breaks inside Chencho. / That night, he supervises the patrol, / he checks the shifts, / the rotation of men, / and prays with a brother from the church. / He says goodbye to him, telling him he will not attend the religious service. / He arrives home and embraces his wife. / Her face on his shoulder, she senses that something very grave is happening. / In bed, both pray. / When they are preparing to go to sleep, knocks are heard at the door. / They wait. / Chencho's sister goes to open the door. / The two hear her say: "No, Chencho isn't here." / The men go away. Chencho's sister goes to her bed and everything becomes silent.

/ Moonlight filtering through the little windows of the house. / Chencho and his wife sleep embracing one another. / The front door bursts open and four masked men enter the house. / They turn on the living room light. / Chencho's wife gets up and runs to see what is happening. She turns on another light and sees the four masked men with machine guns positioned throughout the house. "Call your husband right now," they order her. / She is met by Chencho's glare from the bed. "They want to take you away to kill you," she cries. He tells her, "Bring me my shoes and jacket." / Chencho goes out to the living room. He has recognized the voice of the lieutenant to whom he reports in Sololá. "Good evening, Lieutenant, sir," he tells him. / The latter only pulls his cap down over his eyes, gestures to the other men and leaves the house. / The three men take Chencho by his arms and drag him out to the street. "Goodbye sweetheart," he says to his wife as they tie his hands. / Chencho's sister, wife, and children take off after the group of captors, / one of whom comes back and tells them: "Go back or you'll die, too!" / The family can see them put Chencho into a yellow pickup truck, which speeds off towards Santiago.

/ In a very fast traveling shot, the camera follows Chencho's wife, his sister-in-law, and his children entering the town plaza, shouting to wake up the community. Over their tear-drenched faces, subtitles indicate: **12:03 AM of the 27th of February 1985**. / Dissolve towards the crowded plaza. The whole town is there. / The church bells ring desperately. / A crowd runs to the constable's house and captures him. / Everyone beats him and interrogates him. / The constable provides them with ten names, fifteen names, all of them on the lists that the town has already sent to the president of the republic and to the *Prensa Libre* newspaper. / Everybody knows who they are. In small groups the men scatter about the town and capture all those on the list. / They beat them, threaten them, interrogate them, take them captive. / Before dawn, one of Chencho's brothers and several military commissioners under his command were already in Sololá. / The base commander admonishes them (in mute). He becomes angry, pounds his fist on his desk, and orders them to leave. / In a fast fade-in the camera opens with a view of a San Pedran who is going to Xequistel for firewood, some three miles from San Pedro La Laguna. / Suddenly, the man slows his pace with a frightful expression on his face. The zoom retreats and reveals, discarded by the side of the road, beneath a leafy tree, the bodies of Chencho and his uncle Pedro. / Both are on the ground in fetal positions, / and their hands are tied together behind their backs. / Clumps of their hair have been torn out. / (In mute), beneath the tall, leafy tree, one of the army agents— in an obvious flashback—pulls a clump of hair from Chencho and another from his uncle Pedro. / Both are tied to the tree, Uncle Pedro looks more beat-up than his nephew. / The agent shouts with the clumps of hair in his hands (his mouth open in mute). / The nylon cords have dug into the flesh of the prisoners' arms. / The agents tie Uncle Pedro's feet and hands. / A piece of his skin and a little of his blood remain on the trunk of the leafy tree. The agents unsheathe serrated knives and / the camera, as if startled, returns to the present, to the destroyed corpses. The skin and flesh opened by knife cuts of varying depths / and, on the temples of both, perfectly placed, the red button of the coup de grace.

/ Plaza of San Pedro La Laguna: / the funerals: / the whole town: / there are reporters with photographic and video cameras: / they interview Chencho's widow who is pallid and speaks as if she were not there. / Soldiers take the fifteen captives through the town towards the Sololá military base.

/ *Prensa Libre* headline: "Army Opens Investigation." / The line in which Chencho's wife states that her husband had recognized the lieutenant from the Sololá military base when he was kidnapped is highlighted. The headline spins around / and another one appears: "Calm Returns to San Pedro La Laguna." / The lines in which the Chief of the Military Zone states that the investigation carried out by the army produced the following information: several people were coerced, and Chencho's widow was forced to incriminate a lieutenant from the military base. The officer also affirms that the investigation has concluded that the murderers of Chencho and his uncle Pedro are guerrillas from the group known as IXIM. / And another headline affirms: "No Lieutenant Implicated in San Pedro Crimes," and the article asserts once again that the murderers of the military commissioners and other townspeople were members of IXIM.

It says that the guilty parties have been apprehended and that they are the same ones who coerced Chencho's widow, that the innocent will be released and the guilty punished.

/ Subtitles: **December 1985**. Some of the released prisoners begin to arrive in San Pedro with apprehension. It is known that some of the others have gone to live on the coast, and that others disappeared after their capture by the army without leaving a trace. / Those who return to San Pedro do not leave their houses unaccompanied. They do not participate in the activities of the community, and they appear to have aged overnight. / For their part, the widows and orphans eye from their windows the ex-military commissioners when they dare to go out on the streets with some of their family members. / They look upon them with anger and pain, and the widows as well as the orphans prefer to close their windows and let the hesitant gait of the ex-military commissioners who have dared to return disappear in the narrow streets of the town, in its sunny plaza, stained blue by the blue suspension of blue light formed by the conjunction that the lake and the sky and the volcanoes make possible and that can be better appreciated from the heights of the side streets of Sololá or from the scenic spots along the highway that winds sinuously towards Panajachel. / From there, the lake sleeps, the volcanoes sleep, the sky sleeps, everything sleeps an intense sea-blue sleep, profound and prolonged, longer than a black night. That's why I say that, to start playing with contrasts, we should begin all of this with a night shot of the lake, and evoke in the spectator a sensation of quietude . . .

Because the guerrillas were going around here needlessly killing people, the army arrived. They came here to these lands of Acatán in their camouflage uniforms. All the army men came with their faces stained. They also killed a lot of people among us. But later, when we had already gotten to know them, they named me military commissioner in charge of coordinating the civil defense patrols. The army men go to your house looking for you. If you don't come out, they have the right to kill you. And they tell it like it is: they say, we come here to kill guerrillas, to help you, to defend you against them. This they tell everyone over a microphone, and then one has to do errands for the army men, bring them their medicines and things. And that's how there have been many deaths among us, but that's why I say the army tells it like it is: they say, there are guerrillas here, they say, and we have come to kill them. That's why we no longer go out, because the youngsters that go out for a walk, the army kills them or takes them to the military detachment. The army hasn't lied to us; on the other hand, the guerrillas have. They have lied to us. Because the guerrillas said, we are going to liberate you, they said. We are going to take power for you Indians. And they didn't do it. On the other hand, the army said, you collaborate with the guerrillas and that's why we are going to kill you, shitty Indians. And the army did it. Those of the army don't mince words, not like the guerrillas who go around saying beautiful things but who also kill—when they feel like it— people who refuse to give them food or go with them to the mountains; still, the guerrillas insist they are fighting for us Indians. But they run away when the army comes. Then we order the civil patrolmen to watch the outskirts of the village, to watch at night and capture the guerrilla forces and turn them in to the army. Because in this village we don't have the right to kill them. In other villages they do, but in this one no, only the army men have the right to kill here. That's why we no longer leave the village, and whoever needs to go somewhere asks for a safe conduct pass, which is what they call it, and which must say:

> The Lieutenant of the Military Detachment, the Head of the military commissioners, the Municipal Mayor and the Committee of civil defense patrols of San Miguel Acatán, Huehuetenango, hereby let it be known that Señor _____ in accordance with his request, has been granted permission to leave to pick coffee in La Mesilla, Huehuetenango, accompanied by his family members _____, _____, _____, beginning the _____ of _____, _____, until the _____ of _____, _____. Therefore we request that civil and military authorities provide him with all necessary assistance.

You also must present, upon returning, a paper from the *patrón* of the *finca* where you went to work. I, as head military commissioner, have a lot of contact with officers from the military base, and I have seen that they too are forthright when they answer journalists that ask them idiotic questions, because they tell them very clearly, look mister, I am going to answer you: Yes, it's true we are killing Indians, but why, well, because there are those among them who are non-combatants but who help the subversives. And that, sir, is a crime. And with respect to what you are asking about, whether it is true that we are starving them to death, what is happening is that if these civilians, these civilian Indians who help the subversives, were given food to eat, were given clothing and medicines to help them get well, they would hand over part of it to the subversives, and if not, they would be in good shape to continue supporting them. Therefore, it's necessary to separate the civilian population from the guerrillas. This is what is called "taking the water from the fish," and it is a difficult task for the army. Believe me, sir, I am a field officer and I have faced the guerrillas, and I tell you that it's not a lot of fun. It's a great national effort on the part of the army to take the water from the fish, taking the civilian population to the model villages to create development poles. Besides, you must understand that the civilian population is trapped by the subversion, that it is prisoner to the guerrilla movement. We have to liberate it, and that process of liberation implies a quota of suffering for these people. It is painful, but any social cost is preferable to seeing Guatemala converted into another Cuba, into another Nicaragua . . .

And when the army speaks to the troops, they also tell it to them straight: Yes, sir, the country expects a sacrifice from you. The life of the *kaibil* is not pretty or easy; we have never said so. The *kaibiles*, sirs, are special forces; they are the elite forces, as one says, the world's best soldiers. The *kaibil* is a machine of destruction that controls his feelings, so this task shouldn't be difficult. First you must kill everyone you encounter in the villages and the settlements in the zones of conflict. You must allow some to flee to tell what they have seen so that terror may spread throughout the population. You must be cruel to everything that moves: women, children, the elderly, animals, everything. Then you must burn houses, crops, food storage sheds. The communities that will ally themselves with the army will surrender in this phase of the war. All the belongings of those who flee—clothing, houses, family, food, animals, everything—must be destroyed, because to flee is to admit that one is with the subversion. Then you must harass the groups that flee and cut off their sources of food so that they will surrender. The ones that surrender are interrogated and the suspicious ones are eliminated. The rest are set free in public and placed in areas under the army's control so that the subversives cannot recruit them again. The success of the army is based on hunger, malnutrition, disease, and death, because then the army feeds them, cures them, and avenges the dead by killing the guerrilla, who is the *kaibiles'* enemy. You who come from the villages and towns where the guerrillas show up and where you are going to have to kill your own people, realize that this is because of the subversion. The guerrillas force you to kill your own people; the *kaibil* is the savior of the country and of the values of God, Fatherland, Freedom, Work, and Family—that's what decent men defend. The fatherland expects you to kill, destroy, and wipe out those who support the subversion, so that when the subversives no longer have the help of civilians you may kill them. It is a very high price we are paying to end the subversion and keep the country free, but when we triumph it will all be due to you, and the fatherland will know how to thank you for it. It should be clear to you that once the subversion is defeated the army will be able to let the politicians make their democracy and allow all to live in peace... But for the moment the war is the important thing.

Now: Attention! March: one, two, three, four, one, two! . . . *Kaibil, kaibil, kaibil! Kill, kill, kill!* What does the *kaibil* kill? *Guerrilla subversives!* What does the *kaibil* eat? *Guerrilla subversives!* One, two, three, four, one, two! . . .

That's why we no longer leave. We're better off here. In the village. Because yes, one knows what to watch out for with the army. Not with the guerrillas. Because the guerrillas promised liberation, and they didn't do it. On the other hand, the army speaks clearly. And it does what it says.

My dear brother Efraín:

I have to report that the people of the Guerrilla Army of the Poor—EGP—came around here to our guerrilla front called The Star (in formation), and they asked us if we wanted to join their organization, and we told them that we were already organized with the Revolutionary Movement of the People IXIM, and then those of the EGP told us that the organization, ours, that is, wasn't part of the Guatemalan National Revolutionary Unity—URNG—that was created a few months ago, and for that reason IXIM didn't exist. Then they left us an EGP flag and told us to fly it in the village, and if they returned and we hadn't raised it and didn't say we were with the EGP, they were going to kill all of us.

The thing is that when the ones from the EGP returned about a week later, we didn't have the flag raised, and we told them again that we were loyal to IXIM and the *compañeros* who headed it. They asked who were IXIM militants, and thirty-two *compañeros* raised their hands, and then the EGP people took them aside and shot all of them. They, the EGP people, tied up twenty others, among them some women, for a week in their houses.

Since I'm the person here in charge of the Guerrilla Front of the Star, the other *compañeros* thought that I shouldn't identify myself as a member of IXIM at first, and that's why I can report all of this to the leadership of our movement.

The Star, as a guerrilla front in formation, will have to start rebuilding itself again, this time in hiding not only from the army, but also from the *compañeros* of the URNG. We have learned around here that in other places where IXIM is active, for example in Barberena, in the eastern part of the country, the Revolutionary Armed Forces—FAR—are the ones who have moved to block our efforts and oblige the people to change organizations. The ORPA is doing the same in the capital, and the people of the Guatemalan Labor Party—PGT—are, as always, not doing a thing but speaking against us.

The thing is, *compañero*, that this cannot go on like this anymore. Our proposal to the *compañeros* of the *URNG* has been to integrate ourselves with them in the area of activity that corresponds to us. It's not right that they are killing us.

According to what you told me the last time we saw each other, you had received a report from the *compañero* in charge of the International Front, and he told you that also in Nicaragua, Costa Rica, Mexico, and Cuba the obstructions against the IXIM are growing stronger all the time and that the Cuban and Nicaraguan *compañeros* are doing little or nothing to settle this matter.

I hope this situation is resolved promptly, *compañero*, because organizing the war against the army and against the other *compañeros* is really crazy. I hope to see you around here soon, and, in the meantime, accept my militant embrace and know that I remain united with you and with the *compañeros* for the shared principles of IXIM.

"We Shall Fight until the Popular Revolution Triumphs"

FREEDOM OR DEATH

J.

Local militant in charge of the Guerrilla Front of the Star
(in formation)

The señor didn't even know that the San Antonio Aguascalientes lake existed until he took charge of handling the properties of a landowner from San Miguel Dueñas. That man's farm was what caused the whole tragedy. The señor was known to visit the farm on weekends. He stayed for long periods watching the dry, muddy lake and the small stream that irrigates the community's fields. It's possible the señor bought the farm legitimately from its owner, but the people of San Antonio swear that he got it by shady means. The only thing certain is that the señor became the owner of the farm overnight, we have to admit with property title and everything quite official. The farm is six *manzanas* right on the lake shore. The señor spent his time coming and going from the Capital to San Antonio, and from San Antonio to Antigua, where he also owned several houses.

The people of San Antonio were day workers on the *fincas* surrounding the señor's property. In exchange for their labor, they received small parcels of land to work for the benefit of their families or the right to harvest reeds for weaving mats. Almost all of them worked on a *finca* near San Miguel Dueñas, and always, for many years, they would go to Dueñas by a small road that crosses the señor's farm. Well, one day the señor closed the road without telling anyone. The Indians protested, but the señor pretended not to understand. To avoid conflicts with his neighbor, the owner of the large *finca* purchased a property next to the señor's farm and ordered that another road be built there. The small stream—which originates in the swamp, all that remains of what was once Lake Quinizalapa— is the life blood of the crops in San Antonio. Year after year the men of our town clear it at the beginning of summer and the beginning of winter. And the stream runs right through the señor's farm. It has always been that way.

About a year after they opened the new road, the señor, without giving any reason, forbade the men from cleaning the section of the stream that passes through his property. The whole town asked to speak with him, and a commission went to Antigua to complain to the authorities, but nothing happened. For two years the stream's waters didn't reach the higher parts of the lake in summer, and in winter the current was blocked by dead foliage.

The community was able to talk with him once, but imagine our surprise when the señor began to read a list of the properties belonging to each person. The man had studied the municipal archives and he could demonstrate to everyone that many properties were poorly registered and the boundaries between them poorly demarcated. The community was never concerned with that, but now that several of those properties were in the señor's name after he had forced many plot holders to sell him their lands and he had fenced in all that he was gaining hold of, the community began to think differently. We organized and hired lawyers; we took our protest to all the civil authorities and to the press. But none of that changed anything.

In the meantime, the señor kept buying up lands far from his farm and fencing them in with barbed wire. That, along with the scarcity of water in the summer and the flooding in winter, affected everyone, but especially the *petate* makers.

One day the señor altered the course of the stream to create an artificial lake, and he set up a fish farm there. That brought final ruin to the lands of the people of San Antonio, who had no other choice but to start selling their lands. But the worst thing was that the humidity bred diseases: malaria, typhoid, and hepatitis, which killed more than one person from our town. The community threatened the señor, but he hired armed guards and bought a fierce bull to keep people off his property.

All of this caused the mayor of our town to start worrying about all the problems this man was creating for everyone. There was sympathy for the mayor among the people of the community because, after the 1976 earthquake, he had worked to rebuild houses. In addition, he himself, along with students from the University of San Carlos, had set about removing rubble and retrieving corpses. In the area that extends from around here to Totonicapán, passing through Parramos and all the area around there, the dead had to be piled up, doused with gasoline and burned because there was not enough time to bury them. The mayor—who was not yet mayor then—stood out for his role in that work, and, when we elected him mayor, he began to rebuild the adobe houses that had fallen down. The thing is that now, when he turned his attention to the problem of the señor, he set about to study the matter carefully. He called open town meetings, and that's how we decided to seek the assistance of anyone who wanted to help the community: the law students' Popular Law Office, political parties, the Peace Corps, the Committee of Peasant Unity—CUC—and, of course, the guer- rillas. They all came with promises and, in the meantime, the señor kept increasing his lands. No one could do a thing about it. The guerrillas told us to organize ourselves and join them in the struggle for total power, but what concerned us was that the river keep flowing and irrigating the people's little parcels of land. Some men from our town took the guerrillas' advice, and we would see a Ladino *compa* from the capital show up around here on weekends. He would take men aside in groups of three, and he would talk to each group for up to two hours. He would leave books with cartoon drawings for them to read, and after two months had gone by, he began to take them to the jungle to teach them how to arm and disarm grenades and how to throw them using stones from the river or avocado pits. More than once I spied on them in the jungle, but I wasn't worried. It was their decision and their Word.

It was about that time that my *comadre*—out of despera- tion—one day grabbed my *compadre's* machete and invaded the señor's lands. No one could stop her; it was if she were pos- sessed. *I go as if I were a man because it appears that in this town there are no men around anymore. We are dying of hunger, the lake is drying up, there is no water to drink and our little ones are dying. Who will help us sow the fields when we are old? If there are no little ones we Indians will disappear. This machete is so heavy, I have to move my whole body to lift it. It whistles in the air as I cut the high grass, it is very sharp, it will help me cut the fence that the señor has placed on the land, cursed Ladino. He and his family come here every Saturday to watch soccer matches on television. He spends his time here drinking with his buddies, listening to Ladino music, singing and dancing, while guards circle his house with their rifles, watching us Indians with distrust. I can barely feel the path. I haven't gotten thirsty or tired of walking. The jungle passes by my side and I sense I frighten it. I think I'm frightening Mother Earth, but if she is fright-ened it's probably because she's afraid that something might happen to me and not because she's been offended. I am going to cut wire, not break the ground without asking for her permission. Only the Ladinos, who don't feel, or act as if they didn't feel, do that. They make fun of everything—even of themselves—they are betrayers and liars. There are also liars, betrayers, and lazy people among us Indians, but as an Indian, one feels that all the Ladinos are like that, they're all the same. My husband says that the* compas *aren't just any old Ladinos. Who knows, all the Ladinos who have come saying they would help us have only taken advantage of the Indians. They fire them up, mobilize them, and abandon them when repression falls upon them. They provide the pretty words and we the ugly corpses. It has always been this way. My papa, who is a* brujo, *is right when he says that the Ladino is the death of the Indian. From the time before the bearded men with yellow hair arrived, he says, the ancestors already knew what was coming upon the lineages, upon the Great Houses, upon the peasantry, upon the Confederations. He says that each confederation had its own flags, its own shields, and that our peoples waged war among themselves. That's why when Alvarado entered the Land of the Trees, the Cackchiqueles helped him conquer the Quichés, and they joined the Tlascaltecans who had come with him from Mexico to fight the Mayas from around here. I have heard all this from my papa when he tells it to my brother in secret. Because I am a woman I can't know all the secrets, but I have also heard (while half asleep) my papa say that it was written that the bearded ones with yellow hair would come, that they were not* Kukulkán-Gucumatz *returning through the sea and through the mountains. They were the dark side of* Kukulkán, *yes,* Xibalbá, *because the lin-*

*eages and brujos had turned to the study of darkness and they liked
to go down to Xibalbá (the very hell one carries inside), not to defeat
its gods, but rather to entertain themselves with them. The ancestors
made a pact with Xibalbá, out of their own lack of responsibility, and
corruption began, and husbands killed their wives for adultery, and
men corrupted young women and girls, and they made war upon one
another, and they had even started to sacrifice maidens—that's why
the Heart of the Sky sent the bearded men to put an end to their study
of darkness, and then the lineages were condemned to five centuries
of suffering. But what do I care about that now? I'm going to cut the
wires put up by that miserable Ladino. I no longer care if I go further
into darkness. I believe that if we are in darkness, we have to make
light with our own hands; just as we entered darkness, we have to
come out to the light, making it, shaping it like a piece of clay in the
form of a little bird, like a finely-braided* petate, *like a well-tempered*
comal, *or like a smoothly-polished* tinaja. *When the bearded ones
had already defeated the people, they divided them up and made
them dress differently, the women with the* corte *reaching their heels,
the men with short pants. And they placed the people in Indian towns
that were close to the lands that the bearded ones stole, which they
called* Encomiendas, *and they made the people work them and then
load everything in big ships that carried the products to the other side
of the sea. Here the only things that stayed behind were hunger and
disease, the bane of all peoples, and our children began to be born
skinnier and slower and stupider. That's why not all us Indians are
alert, because we don't eat well. Our only salvation is* ixim, *the corn
that we mix with beans and an egg or two the hens provide. But, apart
from that, there are only* ichíntal, *only squash. We eat only common
grasses, tortilla with salt and chile, water with chile for the cold,
water from boiled corn cobs, corn silk water for illness—that's how
we get along. Now I can see the wire of the fences just beyond that hill.
I sweat but do not feel the heat; my feet raise dust, but I do not feel
the ground. I think many things and feel that I think them before
enough time has passed to think them. I pass the machete to my left
hand because I'm going to knock down the poles with my right hand.
Then I'm going to cut the barbed wire. I'm just about there . . . now . . .*

Who is coming? It's him, yes, the señor. He comes looking like a tough bully because I entered his land without permission. He comes to confront me, and he comes alone; he brings no guards with him. Now he is going to hear my mouth. I barely notice the time pass. I saw him approach and now I am facing him. He is before me and I shout at him. I pass the machete in front of his face and I can see that he is scared, cursed Ladino. I am thinking in my language but I'm shouting at him in Spanish. I tell him that these lands belong to the community and that he is a shameless thief who is stealing them. I tell him to get out of my way because I'm cutting the wires and if he is not careful I'll cut him too. My soul, my life, my body, are all working at the same time: my soul, my life, and my body, and my *comadre* set about cutting the wires and the señor went back to his house kicking up stones because he left in such a fury. But a few days later more guards arrived to protect his property, and he put up fences again. *I felt the way my ancestors had felt, I think, with power in my hands, the vibration of the tempered blade of the machete. I had felt like sinking it into the señor's belly up to where its blade reads "Collins." I return to town, I walk in the forest, I feel that I am lighter, I feel that I could die now and it wouldn't bother me, I feel like I am a person, I feel that I'm the equal of any Ladino woman. Then I enter my house, then I sit next to the extinguished oven, then I stick my feet in the cold ashes, then I look out and then the whole forest—the trees and the flowers—seem to love me as I love myself, then I feel that for this moment alone life is worth living, then I look at a group of Lords beneath the trees who suddenly turn into Lords of antiquity and then those Lords beneath the trees smile at me and nodding their heads approve of what I have done,* then the community requested a hearing with the governor of Sacatepéquez: telephone calls, telegrams, public ceremonies, denunciations, ministries, offices, agencies, lawyers, lawyers, lawyers, and nothing. A few months later we sent a petition to the President of the Republic demanding a response within seventy-two hours. Nothing happened. The community was ready to attack. Tempers soared. There were speeches, open town meetings, discussions—the people were very angry. My *comadre* bucked up courage and asked if there were no longer any men in the town. One day, when the whole community was tidying up the cemetery, we saw an engineer taking land measurements. A carpenter accompanied him to put up a gate, right in front of the gate to our cemetery, which would mark the entrance to the señor's farm. The people couldn't stand it any longer. Then the mayor himself said that we could no longer sit still with our hands crossed, that they were going to make us Indians disappear, that we had to act. And that's how, suddenly, almost without thinking about it, we all began to walk boldly the path towards the señor's farm: *it's great to see the Indians so involved, the stomping of sandals on the rocks, split heels on the dust of the road, machetes cutting wire fences. The people walk in a straight line knocking fences down as they pass. Nothing stops them. Their sombreros fly off but they don't stop to retrieve them. They keep walking with machetes in hand. I know what they are feeling. They feel the way I did when I faced the señor and I cut the fences. They go along knocking down fences; others put them in their right place, as God mandates, as it says in our deeds from colonial times. We are recovering some twenty-five manzanas of our land. We reach the wall that dams the stream and the people start knocking it down. The women grab stranded fish and carry them off alive in their skirts. The small lake quickly empties and the stream begins to flow joyfully, dancing. It follows its course irrigating the communal lands. All the men are glowing; they are blushing out of sheer happiness. They are sweating, the veins on their hands look like they are about to burst as they dispose of the last fence. We all return to town because the señor's farm is empty. I go along thinking that this matter is not over yet and that the señor is going to think up some trick against us, especially since it seems that someone has poisoned his wild bull,* and sure enough a few days later the mayor received news that in Antigua a lawsuit against him for damages to the señor's property was flourishing, and so one morning a red pick-up truck came into town raising clouds of dust. The men on watch signaled for it to stop but someone fired several shots from the vehicle, which headed towards the señor's farm. The mayor was notified and he ran to the church. The bell was rung and the whole community met in the atrium. There he said that they wanted to kill him, and the people went into action once again. They armed themselves with machetes, hoes, sticks, stones, and a few old carbine rifles from the time of the Liberal Revolution, and they marched towards the señor's farm to capture the secret police agents from the red pickup truck. I was one of those leading the group: *the farmhouse becomes larger; it approaches us. Suddenly the flash from a gun is seen in one of the windows and then a shot is heard, Several shots follow the first; it's the señor's son shooting at us with an M-16 rifle (I know the sound of that rifle because I did military service when I was eighteen years old. I know the sound of the Galil as well, which the army uses a lot since Carter cut off military aid to Guatemala and Israel began to supply it). The group of Indians surrounds the house. I am one of those who are up front. Suddenly I find myself standing behind the big house and I can see the girl, the señor's daughter, and the farm's foreman huddling in the kitchen. The three of them are alone in the big house. The people in the pickup have disappeared. My Indian companions have started to burn the buildings surrounding the house: the stalls, the corrals, and the garage. They also set fire to the red pickup truck. I'm climbing onto the roof of the house. I walk carefully so they won't hear my steps. I reach the front. I see the señor's son holding the rifle in his hands and shooting at us Indians. I pull my machete from its sheath and zap, take that, you son-of-a-bitch, I deliver a deep cut to his arm. He screams and drops the rifle. I signal to my fellow Indians and they all approach. They break the doors and windows and enter the house. When I get down from the roof I shout at my companions to stop. Besides the wound that I gave him, the señor's son has a machete cut on his head and another above his left eyebrow. His whole eye looks swollen like it's about to burst. His arm was also broken by my blow. We Indians grab the girl and the foreman and, along with the señor's son, take them to town. There in the plaza are the three of them crying. The people accuse them of assaulting the community. I have the M-16 in my hands; I know it as well as the Galil. Because of the seriousness of his wounds, the people decide to send the señor's son to the hospital in Antigua, the city of streets paved with stones, the city*

*of stone arches and stone domes, the city of secret passageways and
dungeons, of cells for mad nuns, of brick chambers full of unborn children, of archways full of flowers and pleasant shade, of the white and
luminous cathedral, of the Palace of the Captains General, of the conquistadors humiliated before the blue volcano that drowned their
pride flooding the city with boiling water, of Doña Beatriz the
Unfortunate, of our first mestizo woman, Doña Leonor de Alvarado
y Xicoténcatl, the governor's daughter, the one in the humiliating
plays of the Conquest performed by Indian actors—Indians wearing
yellow wigs, Indians wearing red wigs, Indians in colored pants,
Indians in filthy loincloths walking the streets, playing war, dancing
the Dance of the Conquest as the Spanish ladies fan themselves and
the gentlemen arrogantly adjust their swords, the haughty Spanish
banner, the core of the humiliation of the Indians, manicured city
where we go to sell our cloth, nowadays made into little purses, back-
packs, little Ladino dolls dressed as Indians, pastel-colored vests (we
have had to pastelize our colors, the colors taken from blackberries,
oranges, apples, and strawberries, from the sky, from the lakes).
Antigua, the City of Everlasting Roses: the rose of Cairo, the rose of
Hiroshima, the rose of Vietnam, the name of the unnamable rose, of
roses pouring from balconies and blazons, of the crying of bougainvil-
lea, of the whistling pines, of the shadow of the volcano over
everything, of the tripping of someone who leaves his patio and stum-
bles upon the skirt of the volcano that begins to ascend by the side of
his mother's rose garden, beside the kitchen door through which an
Indian woman exits with a steaming breakfast. The city of the conquistadors, of the Creoles, of the chroniclers, of the inventors of today's
history, of the negators of yesterday's history, of the Antiguans. The
city where the Indians come down to discover that they are Indians,
that there exists another kind of people who call themselves Ladinos
who live in a magic world in which things move all by themselves
without any beasts pulling them, in which people talk from one place
to another without seeing each others' faces, in which everyone dress-
es in strange clothes and watches in color what happens on the other
side of the sea. Antigua: the city of the Arch of Santa Catalina,
beneath which the bleeding Jesus Christ passes and the women follow*

him on his way to Calvary. Jesus of the red tunic emerges from the incense that rises to Heaven and almost erases the volcano from the horizon . . . and he passes . . . the Indians behind him, the musicians behind him . . . the Romans behind him . . . the Jews behind him . . . and the Ladino closes his door and returns to his television set to watch Ben Hur *or* The Ten Commandments. *Antigua: the city of crafts-men of bronze, gold, glass, wood, stone . . . the Water Volcano watches you, city of buried fingernails, testimony to the greatness and misery of Spain, to the misery and greatness of Guatemala, that of the men on horseback, those of four legs and two heads, of the mirrors, the swords and cannons and firearms, those with fire in their hands, the condemners to death, the rapers of Indian women, the decapitators of* brujos *and seers and men and women and children and elders, those who burned the codices, those with the raised cross and the lowered sword, those we Indians confused with gods five hundred years ago disregarding the prophesies. Because they were not* Kukulkán, *they were not* Kukumátz, *they were* Xibalbá, *and Antigua is the city of old* Xibalbá—*that's why it is so pretty. Antigua: the city of Friar Bartolomé de las Casas who they say defended the Indians although what he wanted was power for the Crown and not for the* Encomenderos *and that's why he denounced the destruction of the Indians. Antigua: the city of Bernal Díaz del Castillo, a soldier from Spain by the grace of God, a conquistador impoverished by the grace of the Crown, historian, chronicler, and writer out of necessity, narra-tor of the Spanish feats because Spain was starving him to death in the Indies and he had to justify his pension, his awards, his lands, his Indian men, his Indian women. Antigua: the city of Brother Pedro, that saint who went mad with love and who said: Remember brothers, that we have a soul, and if we lose it we shall never recover it. We Indians and Ladinos at war say: Remember brothers that we have one weapon, and if we lose it we shall not recover it. We are far from* Kukulkán *and Brother Pedro de San José Betancourt, the one who picked up sick people from the streets and took them to his little hos-pital, that hospital in Santiago de los Caballeros, Antigua's hospital, the one to which the community decides to take the señor's son because it looked like his eye was going to fall out. One thousand five hundred*

*of us Indians wait in the plaza for the authorities to arrive. I was wak-
ing up when I heard the motors of two cars entering the town raising
dust; it was the police. People reacted and drove away the occupants
of the vehicles with stones. The mayor, knowing that the police would
return and that then there would be a lot more of them, directed the
people not to move from the plaza and ordered the girl and foreman
jailed. And yes, at around nine in the morning, besides several dilapidated cars without license plates, two buses arrived with some sixty
men from the platoon. They were led by their chief, Manuel de Jesús
Valiente Téllez. The mayor had ordered fifty Indians to dig trenches
around the outskirts of town and raise barricades. The police captured
many of them as well as onlookers and passers-by who were walking
along the road. They grabbed twenty people and prepared to enter the
plaza. In front of the policemen came two priests from Antigua in their
robes asking the Indians to remain calm and to cooperate—like Friar
Bartolomé de las Casas. All of a sudden the voice of Valiente Téllez—
like that of Pedro de Alvarado—was heard from an electric
loudspeaker as tear gas canisters began to fall upon the crowd—like
the cannon balls of the conquistadors. The people dispersed, some fleeing to their houses and others to the forest to mount resistance for who
knows how long—just like in the times of the Conquest. Then Valiente
Téllez entered the jail, where the mayor was. Téllez had a rifle in his
hand and two pistols at his waist. There in the jail he struck the
mayor's face and humiliated him—as Alvarado did with the Lords of
Utatlán—and he released the two prisoners, the girl and the foreman.
He put them in a car and they were taken away. Valiente Téllez seized
the M-16 that I had turned over to the mayor, so we lost the firearm
never to recover it again, and that's how the evidence that could have
incriminated the señor's children disappeared. When they left, the
police took away two more men at random. In all, they took away
twenty-two men. The next day, the newspapers of the capital city read:
"Enraged Indians Burn Farm and Attack Citizen." And the people of
our town began to try to figure out what they could do to free the twenty-two prisoners. In the meantime the wives of the captives cried with
their little children because they thought their husbands would never
again return. Most of the twenty-two were tortured. We spoke to a*

very young lawyer from Antigua who accepted charge of the case. About a month later they freed all of them but they returned lame or with a dead arm or without fingernails and so on, and they told the community that they had to confess the names of all who had in one way or another participated in the assault on the señor's farm. That was tough because from then on everyone expected to be captured; we all thought we were on the authorities' list. I hid first in Dueñas and then in Ciudad Vieja, and the mayor and other friends kept me informed about how things were going. It happened that through the law students of the University's Popular Law Office the community had made contact with the guerrillas, then with the passing of time painted slogans began to appear on the walls of houses, which read: "Out with the thief!" or "Power to the CUC and the people!" or "The people united will never be defeated!" And then, yes, the army began to patrol the Department of Stacatepéquez more intensely. Up until then it had been the police that dealt with the San Antonio problem, but when the guerrillas arrived painting slogans and wanting it to look like they had influenced the community to do what it had done, then it was the army that came down on us and things got really rough. And that's how time passed and the village of Chimachoy, which is surrounded by the lands of people from San Antonio, was bombed, they say in order to sweep out the subversives. The army ordered the people of Chimachoy to leave. The men left and the women and children set up a refugee camp on the outskirts of San Antonio. And the army went there and tortured the children so that their mothers would tell them where their husbands were; they cut off the little ones' ears and they broke their little fingers and arms. Those painted slogans on the walls were our misfortune. I was the first one they grabbed because I was listed as the leader of the assault on the señor's house and the army knew I had cut his son's arm and broken it. The first time they tried to capture me was one night right in town, but I saw them in time. It was a group of civil patrolmen from Alotenango. I ran to the church and climbed the bell tower. There I rang the bell as hard as I could and all the people came out. That's how I saved myself that time, but it was already written that they were going to kill me because one afternoon all the troops arrived in the plaza and an officer announced through a loudspeaker that the town should turn me in because I was a Communist. What was I to do? I myself stepped forward and they took me away. I was hanged by my hands and feet—they had already torn out both my eyes with a tablespoon and they had broken all my fingers and toes with a hammer when, during one of the electric shocks that they were giving me on my genitals, I left . . . or rather, I went away. Well, I died. I realized it because suddenly all the pain stopped; nothing hurt and nothing bothered me. I could see the torturers sweating and also that sack of bones that had been me hanging from a pole, almost touching the ground, between two benches, and I realized that, with slight movements of my belly button, I could move from one side to the other and I could fly or simply think that I wanted to be somewhere else and suddenly I was there. I had no feet to walk on nor did I need them, and I could see everything—the town and the barracks—and I knew who they were going to kill after they killed me. The mayor would be the first. Then I decided to accompany him all the time until he was on this side and that's what I did. And what happened was that he was coming from the capital on a bus on the fifth of December. The sky was very blue and the people's skin was ashen colored from so much cold and wind. The mayor suddenly sees that a pickup truck is right next to the bus and is following it closely. The bus climbs to San Lucas, where it gets colder, and then quickly begins to descend the Las Cañas grade to Antigua, passing by the ravines where so many other buses full of Indians have fallen. The Water Volcano meanders along with the bus; it emerges and disappears between the hills, between the mountains, erect and asleep against the blue morning sky. The bus arrives at Antigua and the mayor gets off and enters the market (I go with him the whole time). He goes in between the flower stalls and eateries and mingles among the dirty Indians: the colorful clothing blended with bouquets of flowers and pots of white rice, yellow rice, meat battered in green sauce, steaming soups full of carrots, peruleros, potatoes, güisquiles, string beans, turnips, pumpkins, and gourds. The golden fish and the hard-boiled eggs and the tortillas and the chiles and the avocados absorb him, swallow him, and the secret police agents cannot follow him. I too go into the eateries. I visit in passing another of my comadres *who with her fat arms and sweat-covered face serves and serves and serves nonstop the truck drivers who come and go from the coast to the mountains and from the mountains to the coast, and she serves the Indians also. The aromas of the food and of the flowers and of the sweat of the Indians whirl vapors which at times arrive mixed with the smells of caramel and mint candies, cilantro, and parsley. The Indians eat with their hands or a spoon—everything with the same spoon and with their hands. They swallow great quantities of tortillas and chiles. From time to time they take a little swig of* súchiles *or* tiste *drinks. The mayor sees the secret police agents leave the market and he eats among all the Indians. Then he leaves and takes a bus towards San Antonio. There goes the mayor, among chickens, sleeping children, tired women, and drunken men who doze off with their heads on other people's shoulders. The bus bounces along the dirt road, and I follow behind, flying, waiting for the secret police agents to appear because this is the day that Death is going to tap the mayor on his shoulder. And there they are; here they come: the dilapidated car appears on a curve and stays close to the bus. The mayor sees it; he sees how it overtakes the bus and stops in front of it forcing it to halt. He sees how the three men in civilian clothes get out. The mayor recognizes one of them; he is an Indian and his name is Toribio. He is from San Juan. The mayor knew his father, who was a fireworks maker. They board the bus and begin to ask for identification. From their bags, the Indians take out their identification cards or their military service cards or their permission and safe conduct passes or even birth certificates. When they reach the mayor one of the agents confiscates his papers and sticks them in his bag, and the other two take him out with his hands tied. They take him out of the bus and order the driver to continue on his way. "Tell my wife that they have me!" shouts the mayor. They hit him on the head and shove him into the car, which turns around, raising dust clouds, and takes the road back. I am there in the car with them. Two policemen have the mayor pressed between them. They talk to him, tell him that he is going to die, that they intend to kill him. They shove the barrels of their pistols in his ribs. They hit him on the head with*

them, on his face. In the front seat, next to the driver, Toribio the fireworks maker sweats. "One more Indian," he thinks. "How much
longer are they going to keep killing Indians." He knows that because
he is a kaibil his companions will expect him to be the one to tie the
mayor by his hands and feet with a nylon cord, and also the one who,
after they all torture him, will burn him, pull out his hair, cut off his
fingers and tongue, rip out his eyes and teeth . . . and he, Toribio, will
be the one to strangle him with another nylon cord. I can hear him
thinking: "Another Indian, how long will this last? The Indians will
never be eliminated from this country—the Land of the Trees for
Indians and of the Eternal Spring for the Ladinos. There will be no
country without Indians. There will be no Guatemala without
Cuauhtimallán, that is the truth. A Guatemaya must come into being,
but when?" In Toribio's turbid mind a bottle rocket explodes above the
blue sky of his village, above the little church where the Virgin of
Conception is. Once again his father's smile appears to him in the
clouds beside the volcano; his spiderlike hands return to braid the fireworks' fuses and his deep wrinkles fill the emptiness of his thoughts,
the blue mental blocks of his memory. One of the policemen breaks the
mayor's nose with the barrel of his pistol, grabs him by the hair, pulls
his head back, and proceeds to smash his teeth with the pistol's han-
dle. The other one handcuffs him. I am with them; nothing hurts me;
suddenly I am able to connect my mind with the mayor's and we begin
to communicate with each other without talking. He is on my wave-
length, with my peace, with my detachment, with my indifference,
and he tells me that he can barely feel the blows. That's why, when the
car stopped suddenly on a turn in the road and they throw him from
it and he falls to earth, the mayor feels almost nothing. They tie him
to a tree and the serious torture begins. I speak to him the whole time,
and he speaks to me. Neither one of us uses words but both of us speak
our Word before the Face of the Sky and the Face of the Earth. From
time to time he lets out one or another shout when they break a finger or they rip out clumps of hair or they burn him with lighters with
the name Peter Stuyvesant printed on them, and then he keeps talking with me. So that when Toribio slowly strangles him, the mayor

almost does not realize it. We keep talking. I see him leave his body and he realizes he is dead, and we both laugh . . .

The mayor's body was dumped at the entrance to town so that everyone could see it. When they took away his corpse, a friend became very indignant and shouted that what they had done to him, the town was going to do to the assassins—leave them face down. We, the mayor and I, were there when Toribio and the policemen searched for this friend of the mayor. They were so dumb that, when he acted like he was drunk and threw himself down in the road, they walked right by him. Another Indian, they must have thought, who fell down from drinking so much guaro. But the second time they went looking for him they most certainly did kill him. They went to his house and, in front of his wife and daughter, they machine-gunned him as he tried to escape. When he left his body he saw us, and the three of us laughed a lot. From time to time it saddened him how his daughter had cried and how she became embittered. "An Indian who died for a dried up lake," she said of him, and he suffered; but little by little it stopped bothering him. The three of us saw how the guerrillas brought a spy to justice, an old Indian who had lands at the base of the Acatenango volcano. The compas disguised themselves as peasants. They went to his lands looking for work and, when the gentleman approached them, one of them pulled out a nine-millimeter pistol from his sack and shot him. As he abandoned his body he looked at us angrily and left. He disappeared in the direction of the volcano there by his lands. And we were also present when they killed an employee of another Indian who had been in the CUC and a councilman for the mayor—the two of them joined us—the municipal secretary, who they went to kill in Parramos, a day laborer whose wife died a little later out of sheer sorrow and who also joined us (the mayor's councilman sometimes cried because his wife now had to go to sell fruit at the bus terminal in the capital, and she would leave very early and return very late, and his daughter blamed him for all of that). We were also present when they killed the owner of the store where there was an autographed photo of Eisenhower on a shelf because the shopkeeper's

*wife had sent Ike a weaving of the kind the Ladinos call "typical"
with his portrait embroidered on it, and then Ike had written them
a letter of thanks and had sent them a photo of himself. They took
this store owner away in a pickup. They killed the young lawyer
from Antigua who had helped us free the twenty-two prisoners that
Valiente Téllez had taken away. He also joined us, and together we
went to see how they killed the mayor of Ciudad Vieja. And that's
how it was until there was a coup d'etat in the capital, which put an
end to the slaughter in San Antonio and surrounding areas. The
death that we missed completely—while watching over the people of
our town and whispering in their ears so they would have good
thoughts—was the señor's. It turns out that the guerrillas—as if
they were going to remedy anything—got him in his office. Two of
them arrived on a motorcycle they left in the street and went in and
filled him with lead right in his office. His soul didn't even go near
San Antonio. We never saw him ever again, and it's a good thing
too, I say, because why would we see him again anyway?*

*Now the people of San Antonio have lost their lands because the
law sided with the property deeds the señor had drawn up and everything passed to the hands of his heirs . . . The people do not go out at
night, they only walk the streets during the day, and everyone is sad,
very sad. We the dead walk along there, watching, doing penance,
waiting for this uncomfortable calm to end once and for all so that we
can go rest in peace by the warmth of the Heart of the Sky that calls
and calls and calls for us to be born again and return to struggle . . .*

T oribio de León, ex-fireworks maker, *kaibil*, opens and reads from his training manual:

CHAPTER 7
Operations and Tactics
Section II: Attack Operations
Page 131, Paragraph 119, Reserves

The reserves (or reaction forces) are retained by the brigade and its subordinate units either within the area of attack or at a certain distance from it, or in both places, so that they can enter into offensive combat at the decisive moment and place to accomplish their mission of destruction.

After looking at the inserted illustration, Toribio writes in a notebook:

The TNT bombs weigh up to 110 pounds; they knock down trees and leave craters in the ground between 30 and 45 feet in diameter. The blasts can be heard as far as 12 miles away in every direction.

The nearby hills, forests, jungles, and mountains are bombarded from the plazas of occupied towns and also from the highways. To accomplish this, cannons, howitzers, and tanks are used, and trees are knocked down for 200 yards on each side of the highways to prevent ambushes. Forests and jungles are burned with defoliants, incendiary bombs, and napalm, which cannot be extinguished with dirt and corrodes rocks. Its flame is yellow, very intense and long, several yards in length, and its smoke is very black and dense.

Great expanses of cultivated land are burned to starve the population. That's why it is hotter now and rains less. The plants do not grow back because the chemical substances penetrate the subsoil.

Besides degrading the earth, napalm mixes with rain and contaminates the water when it drenches the fields. They say it will take from 30 to 50 years of intense treatment for the land to be productive again. The soil mineralizes and erodes.

The degradation of plant life kills the wild fauna. The craters formed by the bombs fill with water in winter and become breeding grounds for mosquitoes, which bring malaria to the people. They say that the pine forests will need 100 years to regenerate. The people are starting to live under the trees, and we are burning the land and the trees. The land of the trees . . .

Toribio picks up his training manual again and opens it to page 177:

CHAPTER 8
Complementary Operations
Section II: Intelligence Operations,
Paragraph 148 (2), Detection Measures

Proper detection measures in counter-guerrilla operations may include the following:

a) Investigate the background and determine the usefulness of all civilians employed by the U.S. Forces and of those of the host country that collaborate with them and of those that occupy official posts. Special attention should be paid to the control of guides or trackers familiar with the location, disposition, and objectives of friendly forces.

b) Maintain under surveillance all individuals known or suspected to be members of the guerrilla forces and their clandestine or auxiliary organizations. (end of page 177)

c) Use flares, booby traps, or ambushes extensively where it is suspected that the guerrillas carry out reconnaissance activities.

d)   Use dogs in conjunction with other security measures.

e)   Clear away vegetation and plow selected areas to detect any evidence of movement through the area.

f)   Give the utmost emphasis to visual and electronic observation. Increased assistance is often needed in the form of visual and electronic detection devices.

g)   Monitor civilian television and radio broadcasts.

h)   Use policewomen for searching and interrogating women and children.

i)   Carry out surprise counterintelligence replacement and investigation of all the residents of settlements where it is suspected that intelligence activities are carried out in support of guerrilla forces.

j)   Distribute photos of known guerrillas or their clandestine leaders for the purpose of contributing to their capture.

k)   Offer rewards for information leading to the capture of informants or other agents that support the guerrilla forces.

l)   Photograph periodically all residents of villages within the area under the influence of the guerrillas and compare these photos to determine whether the population has increased or decreased during intervening periods.

m)   Distribute highly controlled identification cards to all residents of the area of operations. In counterguerrilla operations, activities are complicated by the presence of a great number of civilians of whom it is unknown whether or not they are trustworthy; it is difficult to distinguish between friendly, neutral, and enemy elements. All possible security measures to facilitate identification of these elements should be employed constantly.

Toribio closes his training manual and writes in his notebook:

When I was a child, my parents sent me to sell firewood, ocote, and grass. Sometimes they gave me 10 centavos for the firewood and sometimes 15 for the grass. With that I could buy a pound of salt or a notebook. I always asked for a notebook but they never gave me one. In the army I can buy notebooks and write these and other things that the people we capture tell me. A woman that we had to torture confessed that in the mountains the women almost always get up at two or three in the morning to cook food, when they have it. During the day they cannot light fires because we detect them. That's why the women have to get up early and cook food for the whole day. The fire has to be put out at five in the morning. When night arrives they can start the fire again, if there's not a full moon. The children do look-out duty, and they go far away to follow the army's movements. When there is someone who can teach, the families gather to learn how to read (because of the insistence of the guerrillas). After a punitive measure, they order us to place banners beneath the trees, strung from tree trunk to tree trunk, that say: "Campesino, go to the nearest military detachment, you will be given food and help for your family. The subversives give you only hunger and disease. Flee from them, the army will protect you." Those who learn how to read will pay attention to these signs.

Toribio opens his instruction manual and reads:

Section III: Psychological Operations

He closes it, then opens it again to page 151 and reads:

CONCEPT

The general program of psychological operations for a determined host country is established at the national level by an organization composed of personnel from the United States and the host country. This program provides the rules that guide each military and subordinate civil group [faded text] with

respect to the psychological struggle for the support of the population which must inevitably side with either the government of the host country or the guerrillas. The brigade must insure that its operations are in harmony with the general psychological operations program for the host country. The brigade will employ psychological operations not only to support its tactical attack and consolidation operations, but also to support its intelligence, civil, and advising operations. Care should be taken to insure that the people's loyalty be directed towards the host country and not towards the U.S. brigade, and that the programs and projects be practical.

Toribio stops reading and thinks, "There is no U.S. brigade here. The chiefs say they don't need the damned gringos to win this war. But there are foreigners among the chiefs. They speak another language. I'm not going to write about that." Toribio picks up his notebook and writes:

In a hamlet near the town of Zacualpa, the troops joined the civil defense patrolmen. They chose seven men and ordered the patrolmen to kill them with shovel and machete blows. This pains us greatly because it is hard for us to continue killing our own people. The same thing happened in the municipality of Joyabaj . They take us to other regions, and to other towns to kill our people.

I will fill up this notebook today, hiding it from my comrades as I always do before I burn it. It's the fifth one. It makes no difference if my words go up in smoke. The weight of my thought, of my Word that I offer to the Heart of the Sky, goes to the wind. This is the only way I can bear all this until my military service is up. I should mention that I am worried about the gringo evangelical Christians that come to console the widows and orphans, the survivors that we have in the development poles. Now no one wants to be a Catholic, and we Indians don't know about these new religions. The thing that is certain is that just as Catholicism was the religion of the conquistador,

Protestantism is the religion of those who control the army. After writing these things, even though I burn them, I'm better able to keep going although I begin to fear what could happen when this war is over, when the Indians that survive organize themselves without Ladinos; but I also think that with all this business of the evangelical sects the Indian leaders are going to be Ladinized. Who knows. At times I don't know what to do and I even wish that all this would not end. At times I don't know who I am; that's why I write these things to burn them later and watch them burn and not forget about my father or my town or that I am a fireworks maker by profession and that all of this kaibil *business will soon be over and I'll forget about it. I'll find me a woman in the capital and perhaps we will try our luck in Los Angeles. I'm running out of paper. I hope and at the same time fear that this war will end.*

W *hen a person is initiated into the secrets he is first subjected to very exhausting tasks. He is forced to walk long distances and change his habits and to do the opposite of what he believes to be right, so that he begins to learn that nothing is right or wrong and that the only thing we should seek is knowledge of* Kukulkán, *the Plumed Serpent. The way this is accomplished varies and depends upon the personality of each* brujo. *My master, for example, did terrible things to me that I'm not going to say here, not because they are secret, but because it would serve no purpose. Once the apprentice has understood that he is not the center of anything, he can begin to understand that he can be the center of everything, but not in the world he knows— which in and of itself makes no sense—but in the world of the energy of* Kukulkán, *which gives meaning to everything, through its light side as well as its dark side. At this point it should be understood that the apprentice has already achieved mental dominion over the things of the world and that he has learned to live renouncing the world, because in some way he understands it, although he understands it as a mystery that can never be explained. At this stage the apprentice has already made contact with or tuned in other frequencies of* Kukulkán, *and he can transport himself to them when he so desires. It is when* brujos *are in this stage of development that people can sometimes see them fly or change into animals, women, or young people, when in reality they are men who are already getting along in years. It must be said that there are also women who are* brujas, *but among us they are very rare and they generally lived in distant times. At this stage the* brujos *can now have their own apprentices, thus maintaining the lineage and the teachings so as not to fall into the error of our ancestors, the* brujos *of antiquity,* **those of the great pyramids, men with bloodshot eyes who could see through the smoke of the altars and the stones of the ball courts, the men with the eye on their forehead, with eyes on their hands, the omnipresent, the space travelers, the benders of time, the men on top of the pyramids of Tikal, splendorous Tikal with its fabulous courtyards and grand roads, with its infinite steps and planetary journeys; men enjoyed great learning until they decided to explore darkness** *and take delight in* Xibalbá, *befriending its gods. When that happened, the Mayan cities were gradually abandoned because the harmony between the peasantry and kings had been broken and the descent of all the lineages to their own* Xibalbá *had already begun. In those days* Kukulkán *had denigrated himself and descended to his hells. He defeated the Lords of Darkness, recovered his sense of identity, and ascended to heaven transformed into the Morning Star, but not without having promised his people that he would return and redeem them. Then the men from the other side of the sea came, and many people confused them with* Kukulkán, *with the return of* Kukulkán, *and then came the conquest and the colony and capitalism and the counterinsurgency. We* brujos *kept our practices secret, transmitting in secret the wisdom of immortality to a few to avoid the error of our ancestors, the* brujos *of antiquity,* the ones who got lost on the paths of Xibalbá. That's why the people protect their brujos from the army, because the people know that the army knows that the brujos have the knowledge of Kukulkán, and the army doesn't want this knowledge to exist any longer, and that's why they seek to kill our elders. But the army doesn't know—nor does it want to believe—that we brujos disappear when they come to kill and burn and that we keep training apprentices so Kukulkán can keep flying and slithering inside us, in the Sky and on the Earth and in our hearts, which continue to be nourished by that sign of the dawn that is stronger than all other signs. And here we are, in ruin but at peace . . .

III

AND MORE FRAGMENTS

The only reason we brujos are mistaken for ordinary people is because we have renounced the world. This doesn't mean that we don't care about the world; on the contrary, the world is a trampoline for discovering other worlds. It is the base without which a brujo cannot renounce it. The repression came here and the army arrived burning the fields and scorching the earth and killing animals and people. The brujos' temple was put to the test because we had to act like ordinary people before disappearing when the army was coming. And it was a great test for the apprentices too because sometimes their masters could take them with them and other times not. So the apprentices had to pass through great trials, for example, being recruited by the army, doing military service, and becoming kaibiles to return to kill their own people. Only later could they come back to look for their master to continue their apprenticeship. This war has been a great trial; it has been more difficult than the war of conquest. I'm telling you this as one who was in both. It disturbs me to see that some of the apprentices are staying in the capital forever and even in the army. That worries me. In any case, now we will have to look for apprentices wherever we can find them and not just among Indians. It is time for the knowledge to spread and win other hearts. We Mayas could disappear and with us our culture, our tradition, but neither Kukulkán nor the secret knowledge will disappear . . . I am going now. If you want to write all this go ahead, although I doubt anyone will believe you. That's why you're better off saying you never met me, you never saw me at all . . .

T he army arrives in waves; it appears on the plain, rising above the lowest hills. From the village a handful of small black points that blend in with the shadows of the clouds can be seen. Covered with leaves, the army rises in camouflage uniforms and stained faces. The army has many faces. It appears by the hill and by the river. It arrives on the road and suddenly has surrounded the village. Beneath the broken sky of early morning or the darkness of nightfall the army approaches. It is they (those from the army) who arrive with black paint on their faces. It is they who appear with torches in their hands. It is they who burn our houses so that the people will come out and the children run screaming and the elders trip on the stones and the women cannot lift their children to their backs. It is they who corral the men in the center of the village to kill them and who lock the women in the church to rape them. They disembowel the children. They pull them from the slings on their mothers' backs and grabbing them by their feet smash them against the stones. It is they who cut open the women's bellies, remove their little ones who have not even been born and throw them to the dogs after splitting them in two, ripping their legs apart like crabs. They appear heading along the road, over the hill, through the plain. What do they want? What are they looking for now? There are no guerrillas here anymore; they all went to the mountains after the first time the army came around. Everyone fled. They took food and corn and the boys and girls, too, our children who wanted to go with them. Then they left us here in our village, alone and unarmed, and many people fled to the mountains but not to go with the guerrillas. When they saw that the soldiers were starting to burn the village and kill all the little animals and that they shot the men who tried to talk to them and make them come to their senses—when the people saw all that, many fled with their children and their old folks to the mountains to save them, because the old people have wisdom and the children are the continuity of us Indians and that's why the army kills the old ones and kills children and leaves the men alive with their women raped and the women with their men tortured. But others remained behind because the army says that the Indian flees because he is with the guerrillas and that the guerrillas are the subversives and that they are bad because they are against the soldiers' fatherland. That's why many remained, so that the soldiers would not suspect them. But it was of no use, because when the camouflaged ones arrived they started asking where the rest of the people were, if they had gone with the guerrillas, saying that we knew where they were and that we gave them food. And we said no, señor, we stayed because there are no guerrillas here. But it was of no use because the army started by hanging several men from trees. The poor men shook with nooses around their necks. They kicked and raised their hands to their heads. Some were able to lift up their bodies and remained hanging with their hands gripping the noose but since they left them there all morning and afternoon, by nighttime they let themselves go so they would hang. During all this time children watched their fathers dying and the soldiers dragging their mothers and sisters to the church, hearing them scream, and if the little ones tried to help their fathers get down the soldiers threw stones at them and spit on them and laughed at them. Or they placed bets and killed them using them for target practice. And their fathers saw all this hanging from above. This happened in waves. Every so often the soldiers would arrive at the village because that's the soldiers' job: to go around visiting villages asking about the guerrillas. But the guerrillas are never in the villages. They only come down from the mountains to ask for food, and then they leave and are afraid to attack the army, so that only the people suffer because of the soldiers. The Ladinos do not suffer; only we people suffer because of them: the children, the old ones, the men, and the women who live here in these lands that belong to everyone because they were given to us by our ancestors. The soldiers also burn the land. They cut down the trees that surround the villages, the ones that grow along the highways and roads, and they burn the *milpas* and all the other crops and pull

up cabbages and onions and turnips. They burn everything.
They pour gasoline on the stored corn, and the *ixim* catches fire.
It burns up completely, including the beans which burn in their
sacks together with the fertilizer and the seeds for planting. The
soldiers make enormous fires, bonfires that illuminate the sky as
if it were daytime. The sky becomes red and the pink clouds
illuminate the little faces of children who no longer cry when
they see all that because their tears dry up like the milk of nurs-
ing mothers. The small animals—roosters, hens, pigs, dogs,
cows, all of them—they kill all of them. They use for target
practice the little animals of the forest and the ones from the village and the children they tell to run. Some reach the
mountains. They flee into the forest, but sooner or later they
have to return to the village. If the soldiers stay there for several days waiting for the people that hang from the trees without
hands, without feet, without hair, to die, then they greet the
children with gunfire and leave them discarded there, and they
don't let the old ones recover and bury them. Instead they pour
gasoline on them and burn them. They burn everything when
they leave: animals, people, houses, planted fields . . . There go
the soldiers, disappearing along the road, on the plain, on the
hill, by the river. They are little black points that blend in with
the black flames of cloud shadows that continually pass overhead moving towards the sea. They have left behind only black
smoke that can be seen from all the mountains where the people who fled and the guerrillas are. The soldiers almost never go
to the mountains; they don't like it there. What they do is send
helicopters to drop bombs on the people and the guerrillas so
they will come out into the open, to the highways, to the plains,
so they will come down from the hills and mountains so they
can kill them. And that's why the people move about, evading
the army like a bullfighter dodges the bull, moving back and
forth, planting a little *milpa* over there, cooking roots at night
because the smoke gives them away during the day, fleeing in
this manner, jumping over bushes, eating chile with or without
tortillas, chile with hot water, boiled chile water for the early

morning cold which leaves frost on the people and on the leaves
when the clouds descend from the mountaintop and soak the
people's clothing, their shawls, jackets, and hair full of ice. And
that's the way one lives up there and that's why some want to go
to the jungle to continue resisting there in the lowlands where
it is hot and humid. Perhaps that's what we'll do in the future.
That's what the people say who are able to go down to look for
corn and beans, handfuls of grain to give to their children. But
in the villages there is no food because the soldiers show up
every so often, in waves, and that's why the villages are empty.
That's why we too decided to go to the mountains with our people to see if here, always on the move, going around in circles,
evading the army like a bullfighter dodges the bull, we can save
ourselves from death. But who knows, because life here in the
mountains is hard. You should see how it rains on us in winter.
Night and day there are downpours that never let up and thun-
der and lightning that frighten the newborn children. The most
discouraging thing is the water that falls non-stop, day and
night. You can't even light a fire to warm up or boil chile water.
So then we all gather there under the trees, the women beneath
the trees, the men beneath the trees, under the steady, heavy
rain, and when it stops raining our clothes dry on our bodies,
or what remains of our clothes, because when the people run
away everyone flees with whatever they are wearing, and later,
in the mountains, there is no way to bundle up and the fathers
and mothers take off their rags to bundle up the little ones and
then they die of colds, and what's the use, since the little ones
die of dysentery because they eat anything they can find among
the rocks. When they are able to have a fire there are no pots or
pans to boil the corn from the hidden *milpas*. The people make
clay *tinajas*. They go down to the rivers for water, staying clear
of the army and the guerrillas, too, because they're always looking for food. They don't plant anything because they are always
busy with war, and the people are able to get containers and
water in the neighboring villages and handfuls of corn or rice or
beans. They grind the corn on stones, and sometimes they are

able to give their children *atole,* but not very often. That's why
there aren't many children around here anymore. There are only
a few young people with us now that have been raised up here,
running from one place to another with our brothers, Indians
from other places. That's how we have been getting along. For
several years we have lived this horrible life that never stops.
When we find a cave we try to stay nearby, because when the
army finds us they drop bombs day and night that make the
children go mad and us as well, and then, taking advantage of
the darkness of night we move to another place. Sometimes
from another hill we watch them drop bombs day and night on
the place where we were and drop napalm and burn the trees
and the monkeys and birds, and the smoke darkens the sky and
blocks out the sun. Sometimes we have seen how some families
get trapped in the circle and how a small group of soldiers
attacks them. Sometimes some of them are able to break out of
the circle, hiding and fleeing without stopping, but the army
traps others, and from another hill we have seen them throw
gasoline on them and burn them and chase the children to cut
their throats before killing their parents. We all watch in silence
and pray to the Heart of the Sky. We feel its presence; when we
look up we can sense that it is angry, that it almost pounds its
fist on the murderers, but we also know that it is putting us to
a test, that only a few years remain until our total liberation. We
Indians accept this punishment in silence as we have for five
centuries, because we know, we know that the murderer will
pay for his crime. Because, who suffers more, the one who
receives a machete blow from the *kaibil,* the one who witnesses
it and later can barely give his testimony because his voice trem-
bles or he remains mute forever or the words get stuck in his
mouth, or the *kaibil* who someday will be alone with his conscience, with his heart that is also part of the Heart of the Sky?
We are all punished, the living and the dead, although we know
that those who die are liberated if they have lived aware of their
death. The bodies remain there abandoned, legless, armless,
headless, their hair full of blood, discarded there among the guts

and hearts of the families. And we the survivors prepare to continue moving, to sleep when necessary to keep going from one
place to the next. The wind brings cold and hunger. The children, whose skin becomes ashen-colored, look at us strangely.
Then comes illness; the children vomit, with their bellies
swollen, spitting worms from their mouths, through their noses,
from both ends. When you have to take care of a child who dies
or you have to bury him, when you hear the moans of another
couple in the forest making more children, you say nothing. You
open the hole, it doesn't matter if it is raining or the sun is shining brightly, and you throw the child in and entrust him to
Mother Earth and continue working the fields or hiding rainwater in the caves or trying to cure the wounded. There are
times when a family decides to turn itself in to the army. Then
council is held and they are allowed to go. We keep praying for
them. Later we find out that they were killed, that the army tortured and killed them, but even so, many families continued to
turn themselves in. We are a group that has stayed in the mountains, but perhaps we will move more towards the jungle. We
have run into other Indians who speak other languages but who
also worship the Heart of the Sky, and we have all learned one
another's language. There have even been marriages between
different groups. We live without medicines, and when there is
a *brujo* among the people, he cures us. That's how we pass the
time, watching the horizon to see when the army is coming,
those black points that become men in camouflage uniforms
with their faces painted, the ones with machetes and plastic
cords used to strangle people, those who speak to us from helicopters through huge loudspeakers and tell us to surrender, that
they will give us food and medical care, and throw blankets to
us from the air so we will believe them, and also leaflets; they
drop many leaflets with drawings in which a soldier lends a
hand to an Indian and a guerrilla kills Indians. But they are all
the same. We Indians are alone. That's why we grab the blankets
that fall and cover our little ones. We protect the little ones until
they grow up and can take care of themselves. From here, where

the clouds live, everything looks small and nothing seems important. That's why sometimes we feel that the soldiers who come down from the sky in their helicopters are the other face of *Kukulkán, Kukumatz,* the other side of the mirror, its black side. But no, the soldiers come from below, from down there, from the military base where they keep their planes and their helicopters, there where the *kaibiles* live, the ones that kill women and children and old folks so the secrets of the lineages will be lost in oblivion and so the children being born will have no memory of who they are, so they will forget their language, so they won't know their secrets or their history, so they will become soldiers. They say the guerrillas are the ones who do all the killing, burning, and stealing, but no, it is they, it is the soldiers that don't love the people—that's why they kill them. Their chiefs don't want any more Indians here. That's the way we see it; the chiefs don't want any more Indians left in the world. The guerrillas, on the other hand, aren't like that. The guerrillas kill, too, but not like the *kaibiles.* The guerrilla executes whoever refuses to give him food. This has happened among us. He also threatens to kill everyone in the village who refuses to raise the EGP flag, and since sometimes people have to hide the flag because the army comes around, then later the guerrillas show up and there are problems. You can't be on the right side of either of them. Some Indians have sided with the guerrillas because the guerrillas say that they are fighting for the Indians. We tell them if that is true, why do they try to force us to read in their language if we too have our own language? Why do they want us to learn to read and write Spanish if we also have memories and can transmit very long messages and know how to keep secrets. But the guerrillas don't understand that; they talk only about some señores called Marx and Lenin who are unknown to us. They don't speak about the Heart of the Sky, the Heart of the Earth. They don't speak about *Kukulkán,* the Serpent clothed in Quetzal feathers. They want to teach us about what they call "compartmentalization," and we don't like to hide anything from one another. Besides we have the tradition of the secret where if you tell me something and you tell it to me as a secret, they can kill me and I will never reveal it, but they don't understand that. They compartmentalize things because they don't trust each other and they want the Indian to be the same as them, but that's not the way things are. They have also told us that God doesn't exist. They must be talking about the Ladino's god, the one they invent and then later deny. We believe in the Heart of the Sky and in *Kukulkán,* his Son, who descended to the hells, recovered the bones of his ancestors and then rose to the sky transformed into the Morning Star, and who lives in everything, in the trees, in the clouds, beneath the trees, above the clouds, in the wind and earth and fire and water, and who speaks to us Indians through all these things that we learn to read from the *brujos.* I can read clouds and I can also read trees, not so much strong winds or the earth either, but I do read rivers and fires quite well, streams and bonfires of all kinds. What I can't read are books. That's why the guerrillas want us to learn to read books, so that every time we run into one of their patrols roaming the mountain, after they ask us if we have food they start talking about Marx, about Lenin, about the oligarchy, about the military state, and so on. So one stands staring at them, but without paying attention. A few boys can understand what they say and go with them to fight against the army, but the majority of the people say yes to everything, but what they really do is start reading clouds or forests or rivers or the rain or the lightning and talking with Mother Earth or with light, which are *Kukulkán's* ways of disguising himself and which only the Indian can understand because *Kukulkán* is an Indian, an Indian god of the Indians, not a Spanish god that the Indians are forced to worship because otherwise an even greater misfortune will befall us. That's why we think that if they wipe us out, all of that is going to end too, and then who will dialogue with *Kukulkán,* with the Heart of the Sky, his father? And that's why we are sure that they will not wipe us out and that this dark night is coming to an end, that *Kukulkán* will fly higher than the condor and the bald eagle—as

in the song of the Ladinos and the soldiers and the guerrillas—
and that we Indians will once again be happy in our lands, in
our mountains, in our pine forests and lakes and rivers, beneath
this immense blue sky whose heart all of us Indians carry here
in our breast. And sometimes we think, what if all of this were
just a dream of a haughty Indian? Because the truth is that we
are putting up with planes, bombs, and cannon fire. The songs
of the birds have gone and some people, too. They surrender or
flee to the coast, although others stay here to resist. People react
in different ways. There is, for example, Doña Concepción Bay,
a little old woman nearly eighty years old. She and her four children ran the mill's motor when dough was prepared for some
forty families. The first time the army arrived they gathered the
men in the center of village and lit fire to the stored corn, the
ixim. It was a shed full of yellow, black, white, blue, purple, and
gray ears of corn, and then the soldiers started to kill the men.
They tied Doña Conce's children's hands behind their backs and
threw them into the burning ears of corn. Doña Conce says they
died with the *ixim;* they lived making *ixim* dough so that the
people could eat and they died with the *ixim* that they were
going to grind to make into dough but now they cannot. That's
what she says when she remembers how they poured gasoline
on the ears of corn and how the flames began to rise and
brought down the roof of the shed. When the soldiers left, some
six hundred people fled to the forest to wander around there for
three months. Up there they ran into a guerrilla column that
they joined, and then they organized themselves in groups.
Some went down to the villages to buy corn, *ocote,* sugar, and
salt with what little money they had; others served as lookouts
and trained the people to throw grenades and open holes and
sharpen sticks that they placed in the holes so that the soldiers
would fall into them. So everyone had his own job, but three
months later when they were all in a ravine in the mountains, the
army arrived and dropped bombs on them. Then they split up
and fled in groups, and the families were separated. Some were
so disillusioned that they went to the coast and disappeared in

the towns there. Others resisted even though there were more problems, says Doña Conce, because, for example, twenty-five guerrillas stayed with her group—almost the whole column, in other words—and the *compas* became desperate when they saw the little ones being born in the forest and saw that the only things to wrap them in were torn rags and that there was no food. Then they started to lag behind us. They were the ones with weapons, but they started lagging behind everybody else, until the people took control of the group and the guerrillas left. One morning their leader gave each of them some money and let them go. "They gave us their weapons and took off for the coast; it was every man for himself," says Doña Conce. She is proud when she explains that her village never surrendered. When they could hold out in the mountains no longer, they dispersed among the people, which isn't the same as surrendering, she says. Doña Conce is now with our group, and she takes it upon herself to tell the children ancient stories on star-lit nights or sunny days when we sit around the fire beneath the trees. People react in different ways. There's Hortensia Cubux, who is the school teacher. She was traveling about the area of Rabinal, far from her land, teaching the children to read, when one Sunday the soldiers started to bomb the hills surrounding the town of San Pablo Rabinal. Since it was Sunday many people had gone to mass and were trapped in the town plaza. Others were in the villages and in the *Diezmo,* where the Rabinal Achí is danced every year. There was a meeting of the owners of the dance, the *cofrade,* the mayor and the dancers. At that moment they saw helicopters appear between the hills and saw the camouflaged soldiers start throwing grenades down from above. Everyone ran. Hortensia—they call her Tenchita—grabbed six children and hid them in some bushes. From there they saw the *kaibiles* enter the *Diezmo* and a dancer run towards the forest carrying a copy of the Rabinal Achí and the money they had collected to present the dance. They saw the soldiers kill the people that came out to greet them; they saw them cut off their heads with machetes, chop off their arms and hack their knees, and all that caused the ones watching great anguish. And then the soldiers left the people there thrashing around on the ground. Later they saw the soldiers burn the houses and pour gasoline on the marimba, the costumes of Chief Five-Rain Ajaw Jobtoj and of Rabinal Achí—Lord of Rabinal—and of Quiché Achí— Lord of Quiché—and of the Tiger Warriors and the Eagle Warriors. The costumes burned in the sun. The little mirrors sewn to the cloth became black, turned into smoking mirrors in which *Xibalbá*—the army—reflected its dark face, its many charred faces, its black face before the Face of the Sky, before the Face of the Earth. There the children in Tenchita's embrace saw their parents die, saw *Xibalbá* cut open the wombs of their mothers and take out their little brothers and sisters that had not even been born and rip them in two as if they were crabs, saw the *ixim* burn. Tenchita remembers a *kaibil* who stood staring at the bushes when an officer shouted at him: "What's wrong, Toribio? Burn, shoot! This is not the fiesta of bottle rockets!" And then Tenchita remembers that the one called Toribio began to light some of the huts on fire. Tenchita doesn't know if he saw them or not but remembers only that he pulled his machete from its sheath and cut off the heads of one of the Tiger Warriors and one of the Eagle Warriors. Everyone saw how the *kaibiles* pursued the Lord of Quiché, the one who asks permission to bid farewell to his mountains and then returns so they will kill him. He was now running with two *kaibiles* after him. Kaibil Balam—the god of war—transformed into two *kaibiles* with their machetes raised, pursued the Lord of Quiché, who kept running until one of them shot at him and put a bullet in his waist. The Lord of Quiché slumped down right there as the Lord of Rabinal hid himself close to Tenchita and the children. The Lord of Rabinal placed a finger on his mouth and the children must have imagined a ssshhh, and they kept watching as the *kaibiles* raped Uchuch Kuk, Uchuch Raxón, the Mother of Feathers and of Green Birds, wife of the Chief, of King Ajaw Jobtoj, Five-Rain. Two *kaibiles* dragged her to a cliff close to where Tenchita and the children were, and Rabinal Achí could also see when the *kaibiles* licked the Mother of Feathers, when they tore the dress of the Mother of Green Birds, and when one mounted her and started to move around, she, with her eyes closed, with her hair pressed to her face and her head facing the sky, with her feet clinging to the ground, sliding in the dirt and dust, and they saw that a second *kaibil* mounted her too and tied a nylon cord around her neck and tightened and tightened it . . . The wife of King Five-Rain grimaced and closed her eyes, and the *kaibil* panted until Mother of Feathers stretched her legs out on the ground and the *kaibil* began to slow down and stood up, adjusted his pants, and kept burning huts, shooting at the chickens, the dogs, and the children that fell one after the other. The *kaibiles* left, but Tenchita and the children kept hiding for a long time. They heard sighs and moans. The people dragged themselves along the ground. The Eagle Warriors and the Jaguar Warriors were strewn about the ground, minus arms, legs, eyes. That's why Tenchita decided to start walking. They waved good-bye to Rabinal Achí and abandoned the *Diezmo* area. They went into the forest as they headed towards the mountains, and she says that while they walked they heard bombs exploding and shouts from far below, and that's when night overtook them. It was two days later that we ran into them. They were dying of thirst so we gave them some water and some of our tortillas. As soon as she was healthy again, Tenchita began to organize a group of people and proposed that we work together to farm the land and go down the mountains for medicines. Sometimes at night she would think that the soldiers had probably killed the dancer, the one who had fled with the Rabinal Achí manuscript drafted by Bartolo Sis, which said: "On the twenty-eighth day of the month of October of the year 1850 the original Dance of the Tún was enacted in our town, San Pablo Rabinal, so that my children will keep the tradition . . ." That dancer must be lost, Tenchita would say; he must be lost in the woods. But later she forgot about that and taught the children to watch out for the helicopters. She told them they had to lie face down and remain quiet. The helicopters appeared between the hills, inviting the people over huge loudspeakers to surrender, offering them food and a warm place with a roof over their head to sleep. The *kaibiles* controlled the markets in the towns in case one of us went down to buy salt, sugar, or *ocote,* and that's why there were people—especially older people—who went to buy things and didn't return. Tenchita never turned herself in to the army, but one day she grabbed the children and with a supply of ground corn started off towards the coast, and we never heard from her again. The army announces in the newspapers that they have released thirty or forty people who have turned themselves in, but they don't say that first they starved them and killed some of their relatives at the military base. The newspapers say only that they free people and that they give them food and housing in the model villages. They also say that the guerrillas are the ones who do the killing, but the guerrillas don't have planes or helicopters or tanks; they only go around asking for food, and sometimes they kill but not as much as the soldiers who every so often visit the villages looking for guerrillas. They appear in waves, either on the road, by the river, or over the hill. That's why we have come to live in the mountains. Here, all of us together warm one another by the fire and sometimes we are happy. Oh yes, people react in different ways, because there are also those that have crossed the border and made it to Mexico . . . Mexico . . . We learned about them from some *compas* we ran into up here in the forest who have brought some journalists or people from what they call Human Rights. They told us that four hundred families had fled from several *fincas* near San Mateo Ixtatán, where there is a very pretty church that looks like it is made of sugar (it has yellow walls and the niches, saints, and borders are pink). The Indians arrive there from the mountains. They gradually appear there walking single file in the fog and they sit down to chat by the basketball court. The army has gone there to talk after attacking the neighboring villages, and since the military vehicles get stuck in the mountains during the rainy season, the soldiers take all of the people's things—armoires, night stands, clothing, everything—and throw them under the wheels of the trucks and jeeps so they can get out of the mud. When the people come down from the mountains to look for their things so they can bundle up, they find nothing, not even corn because they also burn the *ixim* and they force the women to make dough and cook tortillas so that the *kaibiles* can eat after they kill a cow or a pig. And that's why four hundred families went to Mexico, crossing the mountains and jungle, in rain and in sunshine, almost without eating, without looking at one another, without laughing, with their children and their elders and a few dogs. There were hundreds of them walking, digging up roots to have something to eat. After about three months they reached the border, dodging the army, which was blocking their way and made them back up and change their route, evading helicopters that appeared like spiders in the sky. Little by little, after having left some six hundred people buried along the way, they arrived in Mexico where the Chamula brothers received them very well, although they speak Tzotzil, and the ones from this side of the border speak Kanjobal and Chuj. But that's not important because we are all Mayas, those on this side and on the other side of the border. Mexicans and Guatemalans and Hondurans—all of us are Mayas, and we all have blood from *ixim*. And that's why, as the groups of one hundred families arrived, the Chamulas in time found places for them to rest before integrating them into their work, because many people die during the first few weeks after arriving, as if they finally get to rest and then they let themselves die. They arrive sick, without having eaten for a long time, and what saddens the people most is being in another climate and in other mountains. From the refugee camps in Chiapas they can see the mountains on this side of the border, and they say that they spend the last hours of the afternoon there looking at the mountains on this side. They also watch the border because the army goes all the way to the camps saying they are looking for guerrillas, but that's not true. What they want is to keep killing Indians, and then the Chamulas talk to the soldiers and tell them to go away from there if they don't want to have problems with the President of Mexico and with the Mexican army. But the truth is that when *Xibalbá*, the Guatemalan army, arrives to kill people in Mexico, the Mexican army never shows up. People react in different ways . . . The Kanjobales try to keep the people in the camps from hearing the radio station, which broadcasts the voice of the soldiers inviting people to return to Guatemala, to turn themselves in and take advantage of Ríos Montt's amnesty, saying that anyone who doesn't return has something to hide and must be a guerrilla. And so the people have gotten used to seeing these mountains from that side of the border every afternoon and in the morning when they get up, and at least those poor people can see that, because the ones that ended up in the Lacandonian jungle have really had it rough: the refugees crossed the border by the thousands—altogether there were three hundred thousand—and the barracks are very small in the Lacandonian jungle. The people sleep one on top of the other, and they have to bring food in with rafts because the *finqueros* won't let the Guatemalan Indians plant corn there as the Chamulas do. A lot of people died because of that. There were no doctors, and they say that some people from ACNUR stole food and medicines, and so did some people from the Mexican government, to discourage the Indians on this side of the border from going to Mexico. Besides, since the Mexican government has never worried about its own Indians, now that more Indians are arriving from Guatemala, how are they going to justify giving land to them to cultivate? That's the problem. Of the three hundred thousand, some five thousand have turned themselves in to the army, and they really have it rough in the concentration camps that the soldiers call model villages and development poles, because there the people have to hear the voice of *Xibalbá* day and night from loudspeakers telling the people that they have been very bad and that that the dead have had to pay for the help the living have given the subversives, and that the living should behave themselves so that nothing will happen to them. The people miss their huts, their white houses of adobe walls and tiled roofs surrounded by *milpas* that grow higher than the roof, because in the model villages everyone lives crammed into wooden barracks with tin roofs that aren't even pretty, without a *temascal* to take a steam bath or anything . . . Oh yes, our people are in the hands of *Xibalbá,* and we all know that only together can we escape from the soldiers and the guerrillas. By ourselves, without the Ladino, we are going to leave *Xibalbá* and head towards the Morning Star. The time is approaching. From this mountain, with clouds at our feet, we hear in our heart the voice of the Heart of the Sky that invites us to remain calm, cold, without hate as the helicopter of *Xibalbá* passes, because the Morning Star and the Evening Star are the same star and they are not the same star. Both of them come out in the twilight, between day and night and between night and day, and they are the same but they are not the same. Because the one of the afternoon is the dark side of the one of the morning; its brilliance is the brilliance of darkness. On the other hand the splendor of the other is the splendor of light. But both of them are the same star, just as all human beings are good and bad, light and dark at the same time, just as *Kukulkán* has two sides too, and everything has two sides, and between those two sides, in the space between one and the other, there are combinations of light and dark that never end. Sometimes one goes from white to black without realizing it—the shades are so subtle—and one is good and bad at the same time without noticing it. That's why the nightfall and sunrise are the rift between two worlds and that's why the Morning Star appears in that tear, because it has two sides, the dark and the light. That's why *Xibalbá* suits us even though it causes us so much pain, because from darkness will come light when the musical scale has bitten its tail like the Plumed Serpent. From pain, good fortune will come, like after childbirth, and out of this long black night the brightness of day will come forth for all the lineages, and finally Heart of the Sky will open its breast so that the Plumed Serpent may fly free in us and we Indians will stop being looked down on and be recognized as human beings that have the right to struggle, and we will be

free in *Kukulkán*. *Kukulkán* Lord of Light, *Kukulkán* Lord of
Darkness, *Kukulkán* Man, *Kukulkán* Woman, *Kukulkán* Sky,
Kukulkán Earth, *Kukulkán* Good, *Kukulkán* Evil, *Kukulkán* Heart
of the Sky, *Kukulkán* Xibalbá, *Kukulkán* Bird, *Kukulkán* Serpent:
O *Kukulkán*, to you we pray and ask that you reveal your will to
us and that you give us the strength we need to be instruments
of your love and your wrath, *Kukulkán* . . . And here we are,
going around in circles from one place to another, planting a
small *milpa* here and a small *milpa* there, evading the army the
way the bullfighter dodges the bull under the sun, avoiding the
army in the rain, hiding, circling around the handful of black
points that later turn into men dressed in camouflage uniforms
with their faces stained. It is the army that rises above the hill,
that rises from the plain. It comes climbing the ravine, fording
the river, descending the mountainside, and it is coming to kill
and rape and burn, and it appears in waves here in these lands
of our ancestors that belong to us, and like our ancestors, we are
still standing, always standing, whether in the mountains or in
the jungles, standing beneath the trees.

When a person dies our tradition tells us to do certain things. But since Xibalbá came down upon us, we can't even bury our dead anymore. Now the men remain hanging from the trees, from the tree branches, and the kaibiles cut their veins and place a glass there, and they drink the blood so that the whole community will see how the kaibil swallows the life of the people . . .

So the tradition has been disappearing because Xibalbá of the soldiers will not let us bury our dead. It only kills people and then other soldiers come to burn their corpses. They kill not only people but also our tradition; they are killing our culture so that the children will have no memory of who they are, because children get frightened a lot, above all when they see the helicopters come down, and if there are some among them who have never seen one of those contraptions, they become mute and many never speak again. Xibalbá takes the voice away from us Indians out of pure fright . . .

Then why should I tell you about the tradition we practice when a person dies, if now our people are crucified with needles under their fingernails. They give them excrement simulating hosts and making fun of mass. They cut off their ears and noses and raise them with pulleys and drop them onto the floor many times until they die. The ones they take alive, they tie up and throw into large holes that fill up with rain water, or they make them go mad, forcing them to listen to dripping water for twenty or thirty days without eating. They tell the ones they release not to say anything, but they do this so they will tell everything, and those poor people go around like lost souls. Converts of Pentecostal groups, they preach, trying to convince others to become Protestants . . .

When a person dies, our tradition tells us to do several things because for us a person's death is very important. But now, with the arrival of Xibalbá in these lands death is an everyday thing that doesn't matter anymore, because our dead are on the ground, along the roads, hanging from the trees . . . Therefore, please excuse me, but I have nothing more to say; this is everything. The only thing my

Word says today to the Face of the Sky and to the Face of the Earth is Silence . . . There is nothing more to say. What for? This is all, señores. Nothing else . . .

Costa Rica, Christmas 1991
Iowa, Fall 1993

GLOSSARY

This list includes Guatemalan indigenous words, Spanish words, and acronyms of political groups.

ACNUR   United Nations High Commission for Refugees (Alto Comisionado de Naciones Unidas para los Refugiados)

altiplano   highlands

aguardiente   an inexpensive, popular liquor made from sugar cane

atole   beverage prepared with ground corn

brujo   shaman, sorcerer

cacaxte   a basket made of wood branches and rope used for carrying firewood and other materials on one's back

Cackchiquel (Kackchiquel)   one of Guatemala's major indigenous groups of Maya origin

caite   a rubber-soled leather sandal

campesino/a   peasant

capixayes   heavy jackets for cold weather

centavo   cent, one hundredth of a quetzal, the monetary unit of Guatemala

Chamula   indigenous group of Chiapas, Mexico

chilca   herb used to frighten off evil spirits

chiquiboy   an edible herb

chirimía   an indigenous wooden flute played at churches and in communal ceremonies

cimiento   the foundation of a building

cofrades   principal members of *cofradías:* religious brotherhoods or orders

comal   earthenware dish on which tortillas are cooked

compa   diminutive of *compañero*, comrade, companion

compadre/comadre   the godparents of one's children

compañero   companion, friend, comrade

campesino/a   peasant

copal   incense powder, burned in sacred ceremonies

corte   indigenous skirt of multicolored material, used with the huipil as part of traditional costume

CUC   Peasant Unity Committee (Comité de Unidad Campesina)

Día de la Raza   Columbus Day in Latin America, a day of celebration of Indigenous peoples and/or the fusion of diverse European, African, and Indigenous cultures

Diezmo   place where ceremony is held; also tithe

don, doña   titles of respect in Spanish

encomendero   the master of an *encomienda* (next definition)

encomienda   royal grants of lands and Indians to Spanish conquistadors and settlers

FAR   Rebel Armed Forces (Fuerzas Armadas Rebeldes)

finca   in Guatemala, a coffee, sugar, or cotton plantation

finquero   owner of a *finca* (plantation)

EGP   Guerrilla Army of the Poor (Ejército Guerrillero de los Pobres)

FTN   Northern Transversal Strip (Franja Transversal del Norte). An economic development scheme which came to be known as the "Zone of the Generals" due to their illegal appropriation of lands

guaro   a cheap liquor, sometimes homemade (moonshine)

hectare (hectárea)   a measure of land in the metric system equal to 10,000 square meters (2.471 acres)

huipil   indigenous embroidered or woven blouse, worn with the *corte,* or skirt.

INTA   National Institute for Agrarian Reform (Instituto Nacional de Transformación Agraria)

ixim   the term for corn in the four main Maya dialects, a sacred term among the Maya; also means food and spiritual sustenance

Kaibiles   special forces of the Guatemalan army

Kanjobal   indigenous group of Chiapas, Mexico

Kekchí   one of Guatemala's major indigenous groups of Maya origin

Kukulkán   the Plumed Serpent; represents the unity of opposites

macuy   an edible herb; the leaves of the *güisquil* or *chayote*

Mam   one of Guatemala's major indigenous groups of Maya origin

manzana   a square area consisting of four city blocks

Maximón   a saint worshiped by indigenous people in Guatemala

melcochita   colored sugar candies

milpa   a small cornfield

MRP-IXIM   People's Revolutionary Movement IXIM (Movimiento Revolucionario del Pueblo IXIM)

nahual   a power that watches over human beings, generally in the form of an animal

nixtamal   corn dough used to make tortillas

novenario   a nine-day commemoration of a death

ocote   a pine wood with flammable resin, used as torches

ORPA   Revolutionary Organization of the People in Arms (Organización Revolucionaria del Pueblo en Armas)

PDC   Christian Democratic Party (Partido Democracia Cristiana)

peruleros   a vegetable

petate   a mat of woven grass used for bedding

Popul Vuh   sacred pre-Columbian Maya text

quetzal   monetary unit of Guatemala, originally equivalent to one U.S. dollar, devalued in the eighties to five to the dollar, currently above seven

Quiché   one of Guatemala's major indigenous groups of Maya origin

quintal   a unit of measure equivalent to 100 pounds or 46 kilos

güisquil   a vegetable used in stews

Rabinal Achí   a pre-Columbian indigenous drama/dance

San Simón   a saint worshiped by Guatemalan Indians and Ladinos

sajorín   sorcerer

sietemontes   herb used to frighten away evil spirits

súchiles   juice made from pineapple peels, ginger, brown sugar, and corn

tapexco   a loft area for sleeping and storing goods

temascal   a steambath room within the house

tinaja   clay jug used to carry water

tiste   drink make from corn

tún   a large indigenous drum used in communal ceremonies

Tzutuhil   one of Guatemala's major indigenous groups of Maya origin

URNG   Guatemalan National Revolutionary Unity (Unidad Revolucionaria Nacional Guatemalteca)

vara   a unit of measure (approximately one meter or yard)

Xibalbá   the indigenous hell, force of darkness